I Never Knew

Amy Iketani

Published by Amy Iketani, 2024.

I NEVER KNEW

First edition. March 2, 2024.

ISBN: 979-8224291632

Written by Amy Iketani.

Also by Amy Iketani

Coming Home
The Last Wish
I Never Knew

Watch for more at instagram.com/amyiketaniwrites.

To my husband, Yoshi.

Every love story is beautiful, but ours is my favorite.

Chapter 1

I didn't get much sleep last night. It wasn't that I was nervous about today, well, maybe a little. I was more excited that the one thing I had been waiting for, that used to be so far in the distance, was now suddenly so close I could feel it. It was a relief to have finally made it to this moment.

I've had this countdown in my head for years and today was finally the day that I had mentally circled in my brain for four long years. It was the day I could finally walk across the stage, shake some hands and then be able to celebrate my accomplishment.

The sun coming through my bedroom window made me drape my arm dramatically over my eyes. I rolled over in the hopes of getting a few more minutes of sleep when I heard my mom yell from downstairs.

"Luna! Wake up! You can't be late for your own college graduation!" Mom yelled.

I didn't bother replying, I was sure that it was a rhetorical statement. I have been late to many things, but today would not be one of them. I sat up, turned my body to face the window and stood up to stretch. It was a beautiful sunny day outside.

It was going to be a long day, though. I knew my parents wanted to do something special for me, but I persuaded them to plan it for tomorrow. Today was for me and my friends to celebrate together. After today there were no plans.

It took too much work to get to this point, we were determined to let the world know we had graduated. I laughed to myself as I showered and got ready. We weren't exactly party animals, our idea of a wild night might involve champagne or wine and then getting some food at the drive thru. Who knows, maybe on this wild night we might even dine inside?

I came out of my bathroom with my hair and make up done, now the dress. I had chosen the blue one because I thought it matched my skin tone the best. I had fair skin, brown hair and brown eyes. This royal blue dress caught my eye when my friends and I went to the Millcreek Mall last month to look for dresses.

As I walked to my dresser to put on my earrings, I caught a glimpse of one of the old photos I had tucked into the frame of the mirror. There were several that I kept there, curling around the edges from my younger years. These were the important people in my life.

I stared at the photograph of me and my dad for several minutes. Memories came flooding back to that moment in time. We had gone fishing, my first time. Dad had taken me to Lake Erie with a fishing rod for each of us. We stood on the bank of the water and he patiently showed me over and over how to cast the line.

I wouldn't touch the worms, those were gross. I was eight and most of fishing was gross to me, but I loved spending the time alone with dad. It was just me and him out there for hours.

Mom probably would have come, too, but by then she had Alice. Alice would have been two years old and would never have listened to directions and paid attention like I did. I was hanging on every word my dad said and tried to imitate his actions.

The photo was of me holding a walleye that I caught myself. Well, not entirely myself, but dad sure made it feel that way. It was as long as my arm and almost as big as my smile.

You know, I've looked at that photo millions of times over the years, but today I couldn't stop staring at it. It was like there were details in it that I had never seen before. Like, who dressed me? I wasn't even wearing matching clothes. I suppose at that hour of the morning, I did. I laughed again at what a sight we must have been coming back home and mom seeing me for the first time that day. Mismatched, dirty and stinky and holding my fish so proudly.

Mom never batted an eye. She took it, hugged me and made me pancakes, the whole time saying what a great fish I had caught. Dad, of course, had ten more that he caught in the bucket for dinner that night. That was a good thing because if they had to rely on my fishing skills to provide dinner, I would have never gotten past the worms.

Mom and Dad were a good team. Shirley and Ron Delaney married after I was born. In fact, I was one before they finally got married. I've asked them about it through the years and mom just says, 'Life got in the way.' I never questioned it further, it never really mattered. They ended up getting married, so who cared if they waited one year or ten.

My sister, Alice, came later. Now sixteen, she wants to drive everywhere. I hardly saw her during the day. She got a summer job at Waldameer Park, so being a ride operator at the local amusement park should keep her even busier this summer. Alice had lighter hair than mine. I got the wavy hair and she got the straight hair. It's weird how siblings turn out. Sometimes I even felt like we were more different then we were alike.

Alice said she would come today to my graduation, but she wanted to bring her boyfriend, Evan. I said it was okay. I didn't have a boyfriend, so he could have that ticket.

When Alice was born, I thought she was the best thing ever! My own living doll. It was fun to play with her and dress her up. Well, it was fun until she started getting into my things. The day she pulled down the wooden horse on my shelf and broke it was the last day she was allowed into my room.

I would still play with her and babysit, but my room was off limits. She had her baby toys and that was all she needed as far as I was concerned. Because of the six year age gap between Alice and me, my parents often had to split up the parental duties. As I got older and got involved in sports or other activities, one parent came with me and the other parent stayed home with Alice. Usually is was mom who stayed home.

My time with dad was precious to me. I quickly became a daddy's girl and I loved spending time with him. Sometimes they would switch up and mom would come with me, but that was only when she wanted to catch up with the other moms. I think she missed getting out of the house and letting my dad watch Alice.

I started looking at the other photographs I had tucked into the mirror's frame. There was one of me holding my driver's license. Dad, as always, was so patient with me from the passenger's seat. He gave instructions and let me run over a few curbs, but I eventually passed my test on the first try.

Another picture showed me grinning with my braces. Then there was the photo of me holding my new puppy. As if on cue, Bear came running into my room and jumped on the bed. Bear was a beagle and he was ten. My parents got him for me on my twelfth birthday. I had been begging for a pet for years. By then, Alice was in school, my mother had gone back to work at the bakery and the house had gotten so quiet.

Bear certainly took care of that! He brought life back into the house and he was my constant companion. I walked him everyday, that was the bargain. I happily walked Bear every chance I got. Since I commuted to college and stayed at home, I still took him for walks through the neighborhood each day.

Satisfied when he saw me, Bear curled up on my bed and slept. I sat down next to him and pet his soft fur. I don't know what I would do without Bear. I applied for a master's program but it wasn't in town. I would probably have to move in the fall. I wasn't exactly sure if I had gotten in, since I haven't heard back from them, yet. There was a lot of competition.

It was my friend, Nancy's idea to apply. We were planning to get an apartment together and live a grown up life in Pittsburgh, but I told her to not make any plans, yet. I felt so unsure about my future, like my life was in limbo right now. Do I want to go on to get my master's degree? There were days when I just wanted to settle with my marketing degree and find a good job in town.

I just knew that I didn't want to make any long term decisions right now. In fact, now that I had my blue dress on, I was questioning whether this color was a good choice. I pet Bear a few minutes longer then stood up at the mirror. I gave a twirl and then stared at myself. There was no time to change anyway. I finished putting on a necklace and bracelet and was starting to feel a little more confident.

I still needed to decide which shoes to wear. I went back into my closet and tried on both my black heels and my beige ones. After walking around the room a few times, I decided the black ones were more comfortable and they would look better with the cap and gown anyway.

Bear lifted his head to watch me, saw that I wasn't actually leaving the room, and laid his head back down. Bear was my constant companion through all my teen drama. What will I do without him? I took out my cell phone and took a picture of him. This was how I wanted to remember him when I had to move out, my best friend and protector. Of course I had so many pictures of Bear already in my phone, but what was one more?

I checked the time and grabbed my purse. I looked inside to make sure I had tissues. I didn't know if I would cry much at graduation, but with the way my morning had started, I was worried I'd be more emotional than expected. This was the beginning of the rest of my life, but it was also the end of a chapter. Endings, no matter what they were, were sometimes hard to get past.

I took one more look around my room. I didn't want to forget anything since I probably wouldn't be back home until very late. I had a tote bag with a change of clothes, my phone charger and my water bottle.

"Luna!"

"Coming!"

Well, almost. I checked my make up in the bathroom mirror one last time. Grabbed a few more tissues and then went to get my black heels. My cap and gown were hanging behind my bedroom door. As I reached up to grab the hanger, I hesitated. They had been hanging there for a couple of weeks but the significance of these items didn't hit me until just now.

This was it. Ready or not. With everything in my arms, I managed to open my bedroom door. Bear jumped off my bed, stood by my side and waged his little tail. I opened the door for him to go out first and then I followed.

We descended the stairs together. Bear, with the jingle of his tag and collar and me, with my cap and gown like a train behind me. Bear ran right for his food dish. I smelled breakfast, too, but laid my bags down carefully on the couch before entering the kitchen. That was when mom took one look at me and already started crying.

Chapter 2

"Don't start crying already," I said to mom.

"I know," she replied. "I told myself I wouldn't cry this morning."

Mom came to give me a hug. Over her shoulder I cold see dad blinking back a tear of his own. When mom released me, dad came over to give me a hug, too.

"We're so proud of you, Luna!" Dad said. "Our moon and stars."

"Thanks, dad."

Alice was already eating. She gave me a nod and I nodded back. She's not the emotional type and that was okay with me. It was already too much attention and I just wanted to sit down and eat breakfast. I was starving.

"Pancakes," Mom announced. "Your favorite!"

It was my favorite. I sat down and mom placed a plate full of pancakes in front of me. I poured the syrup and dug in. I was careful to not get the usual drips of syrup on my shirt, or dress, today. Mom and dad both sat down with their own plates and we all ate breakfast together. This was a rare occurrence, since everyone usually had places to be every day.

Mom took the day off from the bakery. Dad told his office that he wouldn't be in today. Dad was an insurance salesman and he could work from home some days if he wanted to.

Alice was out of school for the summer and her job at the amusement park didn't start until next week. We all ate in silence with occasional looks at each other. Mostly they were all looking at me, but it didn't matter, I wanted to remember this moment.

We were a close family, for the most part. I legitimately liked spending time with each and every one of them. Even on her off days, mom loved baking. I enjoyed helping her in the kitchen trying new recipes or just making old favorites.

Dad and I didn't fish together much anymore. Now we liked riding bikes around Presque Isle State Park and feeding the ducks. If it was hot enough, we may even go for a swim at the beach. Some of my best memories with him now were just taking a walk with him and Bear.

With Alice, we mostly hung out in my room. She liked going through my closet and borrowing my clothes. She would ask me about boys and I would tell her what I knew, which wasn't much but she didn't know that. She thought Chad and I were a couple.

"No way!" I would answer her. Chad was the boy next door, literally. He was a year older than me, so he graduated last year. We all went to it because my parents said that was what neighbors did. We both grew up here, so we've known each other our whole lives. I guess that was why I have always put him in the 'friend' category and never thought of him as anything else.

Chad and I have spent so much time together that he was probably my best friend. He was the one I could go to for advice or just to hang out. He didn't even have a dog but would walk with me when I took Bear out. Chad was just always there. He was another person I didn't know what I would do without.

"Do you want some coffee?" Alice asked me. She was already done eating and was up making herself a cup.

"Sure," I replied.

Alice handed me a hot cup of coffee after making her latte or whatever fancy drink she mixes up. I finished my pancakes and was sipping my coffee when I heard my phone start vibrating on the table. I've had it on silent all morning because all of my friends messaging in the group text were getting on my nerves.

Everyone was now looking at my phone, so I picked it up to take it into the other room.

"Sorry," I said as I stood up. "I probably should see what they want."

It was just drama. I decided that after today I was taking myself out of the group text. There were only a few friends I planned on keeping in touch with and we could text each other, I didn't want or need everyone else's drama. I scrolled through all of the texts that were just from this morning and rolled my eyes. Really? One text was asking if they should curl their hair or not. Another sent a dozen pictures asking what necklace they should wear. I didn't want to deal with that.

I put the phone back in my purse and returned to the kitchen.

"I'm going to head over to Trish's house now. That's where we are all meeting before heading to the ceremony."

Mom and dad both gave me hugs, again. They would meet me there, along with Alice and Evan. I waved goodbye and headed towards my car. As I was backing up, I saw Chad on his front porch. I honked my horn and waved at him and he waved back.

When I pulled into Trish's driveway, I saw that Nancy and Jenny were already there. I knocked on the door and Trish let me in. Her mom was sitting on the recliner in the corner of the living room. She was bundled up in blankets even though it was May and about seventy degrees outside.

I walked over to give her mom a hug, careful not to squeeze too hard. She was pale and fragile. She had been on chemo for months and was just finishing up her treatment. This was the reason we all met at Trish's house, her mom wouldn't be coming to the ceremony. It would be too difficult and she would get too tired. We all sat in the living room and talked while Trish made sure her mom had everything she needed while she would be gone.

"Oh, don't worry about me," her mom said. "Your dad will be home soon."

"I know," Trish replied as she placed her water, the remote and telephone by her side.

Trish was her mom's evening caregiver. There was a nurse that came during the day, but she took over at night. Usually that type of experience would lead someone towards the medical field, but not Trish. She didn't want anything more to do with medicine. While finishing college took most of her attention and energy, she also managed to get her real estate license. So she not only will graduate with a business degree, she will be a realtor and start her new career in a couple of weeks.

Trish always wanted to stay in Erie, and she was so excited to start. We were all happy for her because it would be a great distraction. Hopefully, her mom will keep getting stronger and won't be relying on Trish as much.

On the couch I could see that Nancy was getting fidgety. We weren't late, but we weren't as early as she wanted. I just smiled. She kept looking at the time and probably wanted us to leave. She gave me a quick look and then paused when she saw me smiling at her. I grabbed my phone and texted her to calm down.

Nancy read my message, smirked at me and turned her phone upside down. I know this was not a reflection of Trish or her mother, it was just Nancy's personality. She liked being on time, if not early, for everything. I saw her take a deep breath and sit back against the cushions. Nancy was doing one of her breathing exercises and it seemed to be working, for now.

Jenny couldn't keep still. If Trish got up to get her mother some water, Jenny followed with a box of tissues, a napkin or a blanket. Jenny was bubbly and positive most of the time. The only time I saw her sad was when she broke up with Todd, or was it Tim. Anyway, she was usually smiling and full of energy.

Jenny was starting a job at the local ABC news affiliate in Erie. She had done an internship there during senior year and they had hired her. I wouldn't be surprised if we didn't see her on the local news in another year. She loved engaging with people and you could tell she really cared about what you said. Jenny had a talent for listening. Not everyone did.

As I looked around the room, I realized that these were my core group of friends. The ones I want to keep in touch with for the rest of my life. I had known Jenny and Nancy since elementary school and Trish since middle school. We played Barbies together, skinned knees together and talked about boys together. We lived through a lot of things with each other by our sides.

Would this be the last time we are all in one room together? Would we all go our separate ways and still keep in touch? I looked at each of them and wondered. Trish was concerned about her mom, Nancy was trying to stay calm and Jenny was getting up for the millionth time. We could get on each other's nerves, but I loved them.

"You girls better get going," Trish's mom said.

I knew she still saw us as a bunch of thirteen year olds, but that was okay. Sometimes I felt like we were, too. Her mother's statement made Trish stand up and arrange her pillows. I knew she did not like leaving her alone, but she wouldn't be alone for long. Nancy stood up and was putting on her jacket. I didn't say anything. I just stood up with her and put my sweater on, too. Jenny was already up. We all gave one last hug to Trish's mom and we went out the front door.

After discussing with each other exactly where we were going and where we were supposed to park, we each got in our cars and left. I received a text from my mother saying they were heading to the venue now, too. It was a familiar drive through town while heading north. The sun and clouds were both competing today, hopefully the sun would win.

Gannon University was a large campus. Not large enough to hold commencement ceremonies, though. Today we were heading to the arena nearby and I wasn't sure how I would find anyone. The parking lot was a sea of people. There were graduates wearing their caps and gowns, parents dressed up and cars trying to get through.

I slowly made my way to the assigned area for the graduates to park. When I turned my car off I just sat for a moment in the welcomed silence. I closed my eyes and breathed deep. I wanted to feel in-the-moment but I also wanted this to be over as fast as possible.

I started eating the bag of goldfish crackers I had in my car. I ate and watched people walk past me. I knew I needed to get out and join the flow to the entrance, but I didn't want to move. It was irrational. I took a sip of water and another deep breath. I stood up, put my phone in my pocket and grabbed my cap and gown.

I looked around for my friends but didn't see them. I felt my phone vibrate as texts were coming through. I didn't know who was trying to message me but it didn't matter, I wasn't going to look right now anyway. I took my gown off of the hanger and slid it on. I hadn't tried it on before today and it felt good. I used the side mirror to make sure my cap was on straight and shut the car door.

I was getting emotional because now it felt real. I zippered up the gown, touched up my hair under the cap and joined the flow of other graduates walking through the parking lot. As soon as I walked in the arena doors I was enveloped in a warm hug.

Chapter 3

Chad released me from his embrace but kept his hands on my shoulders.

"Chad, I didn't know you were coming!"

"I wouldn't miss this for the world, Luna!" Chad replied. "Plus, you came to mine. It was only right."

Of course, Chad felt it as an obligation. But the way he looked at me was different somehow. He gave me another quick hug and then I saw my parents. They were both smiling but mom was holding back tears. Alice and Evan were behind them. I had to pose for photographs with them and then with Alice. They even wanted one with me and Chad.

"I want a copy of that one, Mrs. Delaney," Chad said.

I was glad to see everyone, but also trying to get away. I was frantically looking for one of my friends, but didn't have any luck. There were just too many people here. Finally, I looked at my phone and saw the last text was from Nancy saying I needed to be at the staging area now.

I said my goodbyes to my family and headed towards the other graduates. I was grateful when I found the room. It was a moment of calm after drowning in the sea of people. As we made our way to our seats, I couldn't help but look around. My friends and I took our own pictures and selfies. When we were finally all seated, we were able to talk and catch up.

"I saw Chad give you a big hug," Trish said.

"He's always had a thing for you, Luna," Jenny said.

"Yes, you're the only one who doesn't see it," Nancy added.

I just looked at them. I've denied their accusations about Chad having a thing for me for years, but after the hug he gave me today, I was starting to believe them. I just kept quiet. Chad was handsome and tall, but he was just a friend.

Luckily, the conversation turned to Jenny's new job and her first assignment. She is supposed to interview the Mayor about the upcoming Erie Days celebration. Jenny was to spend most of her early days helping out in background, so any chance to be in front of the camera was exciting.

Nancy asked me if I heard back from the masters program, yet. I told her I hadn't. It was making me very nervous and I hated to keep her plans for moving on hold indefinitely. It wasn't fair to her. I decided that I would tell her later that if I don't hear by the end of the month, to go ahead without me. I would figure it out later.

Trish was video calling her mother. Her dad was home now, too. We all said, 'hi' and I could tell she was already crying. I searched the crowd for my own family. I thought I spotted them, but it was a false alarm. I knew what section their tickets were in, but I couldn't see them until I spotted Chad's red sweater. I smiled at the thought of my whole family here watching me, even Chad.

The actual commencement ceremony took a long time. When it was finally our turn to stand and line up, we all started to get excited. Everything after that was a blur until I stepped up on the stage and heard my name.

"LUNA GABRIELLA DELANEY."

I just remember walking, shaking hands and taking a leather bound cardboard from someone. I might have waved in my family's direction, I don't remember. I just knew I kept walking until I went down another set of stairs and had my picture taken. When we were all back in our seats, we were ready to get out of here.

"We need to celebrate!" Trish said.

This was answered with shouts of joy. The rest of the ceremony went by fast. We discussed different places to go and eventually decided to meet at a bar on the bay to celebrate. After meeting up one last time with our families, we changed clothes and left.

The rest of the evening was filled with food, drinks and laughter. Stories were brought up that both embarrassed us and made us laugh. We had a strong friendship and bond that I knew in my heart would never change.

"Let's go somewhere!" Jenny shouted.

"I don't think we should be driving right now," I replied.

This made Jenny laugh and shake her head. "No, no, no. I mean a trip, this summer."

"Yes!" Agreed Nancy. "Cedar Point."

"No, bigger!" Jenny answered.

"New York City," I said.

"No, farther!" Jenny replied.

"Disney?" Trish asked.

"Mexico!" Jenny said.

We all toasted our glasses to Mexico and started thinking about the possibility. It would have to be at the end of the summer, Trish and I didn't have passports but if we applied now, we could have them in six weeks. I have always wanted to get a passport, but never had the excuse to get one. Jenny would ask for the time off and Trish would just pray her mom got stronger by then.

With the mention of Trish's mom, we all became quiet.

"Did you guys all do those genetic test kits I gave you?" Trish asked the group.

Last Christmas, when her mom was at her sickest, the doctor recommended that Trish take a genetic test to see if she had the particular cancer gene that her mother had. When her results came back positive, she ordered one for all of her friends.

'It was better to know,' that was what the doctor told Trish. Everyone had done the kit, sent it in and had gotten their results. Except for me. I don't know why. It didn't seem like a big deal at the time. Part of me didn't want to know if I had some gene mutation that might give me a problem in the future. It was like I was looking for problems that I didn't need. What if it told me I had something? Or I found out disturbing news about my future?

"But it's not just a genetic test for diseases. It has a whole ancestry part that lets you track your family tree and where you're from." Trish said.

My tree would be so boring. I already knew my mother's side was mostly German and my dad's side was mostly Irish. But I promised her I would do it. This made her smile even if she wasn't totally convinced that I would. The others were starting to discuss what they found in their family trees, but I looked at my phone when I got a text.

"Congratulations, again." It was Chad. I was really starting to question whether he really did see me as more than a friend.

"Thanks." I texted back. I put the phone back in my pocket and yawned. It was late. We agreed to keep planning our trip to Mexico and meet up again next week. I had a lot to do before then. We all said our goodbyes and headed home. I blasted the radio with the windows down to stay awake. There was no one on the streets. I could have been driving on the moon for all I knew.

As soon as I pulled into the driveway I was wide awake. I tiptoed through the house trying not to make any noise. I showered, put on my pajamas and opened my laptop. I researched what I needed for a passport, wrote down a list and decided to get it all done tomorrow. I looked for the genetic test kit. It took a bit of digging in the closet and under the bed, but I finally found it. Trish would be happy that I was finally doing it.

The instructions were pretty straight forward. It only took ten minutes. I sealed up the box and set it next to my list. Feeling accomplished, I went downstairs to get some water. Bear followed me down and whined at the door.

"You want to go out now?" I whispered. The house was quiet, everyone was asleep. I put on a jacket, sandals and clipped the leash on Bear's collar. As soon as I opened the door, he ran to the grass. I had my phone with me and looked at the time. What a way to end my day, waiting for my dog to poop in the middle of the night.

I didn't notice that after I texted, 'thanks' to Chad, he had responded. I automatically looked up to his window and was surprised to see the light still on. It was after midnight.

'I'm so proud of you,' Chad had texted. 'I'd like to take you out sometime to celebrate.'

While still waiting for Bear to finish his business, I texted Chad back, 'I'd like that'.

The reply was instant. 'Are you up?' Chad asked.

'I'm outside with Bear,' I texted.

A minute later Chad came out his front door and walked over. He was wearing a jacket with pajama pants and slippers.

"Hi," he said.

"Hi."

"So, can I take you out tomorrow night for dinner, to celebrate?" Chad asked.

"As friends, right?" I replied with a smile.

Chad hesitated. "Of course."

"Well, I promised my parents they could take me out tomorrow, so maybe the next day?" I asked.

"Sounds great," he replied.

We sat there in silence for a few minutes just sitting on my top step, shoulder to shoulder watching Bear dig in the grass.

"So what are your plans now?" Chad asked. He already had a job at the bank as one of the loan officers.

"No plans right now," I answered. "Things are literally up in the air. I'm still waiting to see if I'm accepted into the masters program in Pittsburgh. Nancy's already accepted and we're supposed to get a place together soon."

"Well, who knows, you could get an email or letter this summer that could change the whole trajectory of your life. How exciting would that be!" Chad said.

I wasn't looking for a new trajectory or excitement. I just wanted answers and a plan. I was okay with boring and normal. I was never much of a risk taker.

When Chad saw I wasn't sharing his excitement, he changed his tone. "Listen, if you haven't heard anything by next month, I'll help you with job applications." I nodded and yawned.

"It's a full moon, Luna," Chad said as he stood up.

I looked up. "It is." Chad always liked to remind me of my connection to the moon. He said that since I'm named after it, full moons are lucky for me.

We said good night and I took Bear inside. Chad was a good friend. We had each other's back and that was never questioned. I knew he meant what he said about helping me, I was now just questioning the motive behind it. I liked hanging out with Chad. He was a good looking guy, but I felt he was more like a brother than a love interest.

I crawled into bed and Bear jumped up beside me. I went back over my day. It was over. The day I had been dreaming of for years was now over. I was officially a college graduate and now I must face the real world. It was daunting and potentially filled with danger and pitfalls. Too much to contemplate when I was trying to go to sleep. I didn't want to think about college, dna kits, passports or boys any more tonight.

I looked at my phone, two in the morning. I still couldn't sleep and decided to look through the pictures I took earlier. I stopped scrolling when I saw the one of me in between my parents. It was a great photo that Chad took of a happy, smiling family. I clicked a few things and set it as my phone's lock screen and finally went to sleep.

Chapter 4

Today the sun was just taunting me. I wanted to sleep longer, but the sunlight would not allow it. Reluctantly, I got up, showered and dressed. I didn't get more than a few hours of sleep last night. Visions of margaritas on a beach in Mexico surrounded by long lost ancestors kept creeping into my dreams. Bear was awake but remained curled up on my bed.

"Let's go get some breakfast, Bear," I said.

Whether Bear knew the word breakfast or just followed me out the door, I don't know. We went downstairs to an empty kitchen. There was a note from mom on the counter letting me know that we were still on for dinner tonight. Everyone was back at work.

I heard Alice watching tv in the living room. I poured myself a cup of coffee, grabbed a toaster pastry and went into the other room. I sat next to Alice on the couch and Bear followed, waiting for crumbs. She was flipping through channels and landed on the news.

"So, what are your plans today?" I asked.

Alice shrugged. "Not much."

"Do you want to run a few errands with me?" I asked.

She shrugged again, "Maybe."

"I just need to get some things done before I can turn in my passport application tomorrow. It won't take long, maybe one hour."

"Okay."

Alice and I haven't had much time to hang out lately. It seemed like I had been studying for finals for weeks and she was, too. Now that we have summer vacation to relax, maybe we could actually do more things together. It was my last shot to reconnect because if I move out this fall, it will forever be different.

It didn't take long for me and Alice to get the photos that I needed and then the check for the passport fees. At home, I was going through the checklist to make sure I had everything ready for my appointment tomorrow when I realized I still needed my birth certificate. I texted mom asking where it was. She replied saying it was too complicated, she'd get it when she returned home.

Well, there wasn't anything more I could do until then, so I decided to take Bear for a walk to the post office. It wasn't far and I had forgotten to add it to my list of errands earlier. I ran upstairs, grabbed the genetic test kit and put Bear on his leash. When I passed Chad's house, I saw him sitting on his porch reading a book.

Chad waved and asked where I was going. "Post office. Do you want to come?" I asked.

Chad laid his book down and met me at the sidewalk. It was something we had done our whole lives, walked together to go to the park, the corner store or to the pizza restaurant. Today, it felt different.

"What are you mailing?" He asked.

I showed Chad the small box in my right hand. "It's the genetic test kit that Trish gave all of us last year."

"And you're just doing it now?"

"Yes, I know, I kept putting it off because I don't want bad news," I replied.

"Who says it will be bad new?" Chad asked. "Maybe it will put some fears to rest. You might even find some distant relatives you never even heard of."

"I don't like surprises," I said. "You should know that."

Chad laughed and threw his head back. His laugh was deep and genuine. Chad was tall, about six foot. He used to play soccer and was still lean. His blond hair, that he used to keep long, was now a respectable shorter cut, perfect for the bank. He had girlfriends in the past, I think even my friends had secret crushes on him, but no one lasted very long. He hadn't found the right one, yet.

I wasn't looking for a boy. I had dated a few times over the years, but I didn't like the drama. Boys can be just as dramatic as girls, maybe even worse. Besides, I had enough going on then to worry about looking for a boyfriend.

I mentioned that my friends and I were thinking about going on a trip this summer. So far we have only narrowed it down to Mexico. Beyond that, I had no idea. It didn't matter right now anyway, because I still needed a passport.

"I only got mine last year, when we went on that cruise," he said.

I remember when his family went on the cruise. His parents actually got along that week.

I was so jealous even though I didn't even know what a cruise was like. I would probably have gotten seasick and missed everything. Chad said it was fun, though, he didn't get seasick.

"What about after summer?" He asked.

"I don't know," I replied. "I'm not just saying that, either. I really don't know. If I don't get into the masters program, I'm going to have to find a real job. I don't know what my marketing degree will get me around here."

"But marketing is so flexible. You can adapt it to almost any field, you just have to choose." Chad replied.

This was the biggest reason I loved talking to Chad, he was calming. No matter the problem or the crisis, after talking to him, you couldn't help but feel better. He was the earth to my moon, the gravitational pull that kept everything balanced.

I had some time to waste before my parents got home and went out to eat. I started doing some research online for destinations in Mexico. There were so many great resorts to choose from. I was going to suggest the Club Med in Cancun, but it really didn't matter where we went, I just wanted to get away for a while. I needed some sun and sand.

I must have fallen asleep because I woke to the sound of doors opening and closing. First mom had come home, then dad. I ran downstairs, I hadn't seen them since yesterday afternoon at the commencement ceremony.

"Hey, Luna!" Dad said and gave me a big hug.

"Hi, honey," said mom and hugged me, too.

"Oh, mom, I need my birth certificate," I reminded her.

I noticed my mother hesitate. "Okay, I'll look for it later," she replied.

"I need it for my appointment tomorrow for my passport," I said.

My mother just nodded her head and went up to tell Alice we were leaving. They wanted me to choose the restaurant, but secretly I knew their favorite food was Italian, so that's where I picked.

The hostess led us to a booth and I was glad when Alice came without Evan in tow. It was a family celebration after all.

We had a nice evening, but I was getting tired of being the center of attention for everyone. During dinner I texted my friends asking if we could all get together tomorrow and hang out. Thankfully, they were all agreeable to a lunch date. I endured my family's attention for the rest of the evening.

After dinner, dad handed me an envelope with a card. I opened it and was surprised to find a check inside.

"We didn't know what to get you or what you would need, so we thought we would let you decide," Dad said.

I didn't know what to say. They have never just handed me a check before. I thanked them and hugged them both. At home, they had a cake for me. This was when Evan and Chad walked in the front door. I suppose I should be grateful that they waited until dessert at home to come to the party.

I took my cake to the living room and Chad followed me. "How are you doing?" He asked.

"I'm okay. Just tired of being the center of attention," I replied.

"Well, can you stand it one more day? Are we still on for tomorrow night?"

I smiled. "Yes, I can handle one more night. I'm meeting my friends for lunch to discuss our trip, but I will meet you for dinner later."

He seemed to relax and enjoy his cake. I did, too. The earth and moon, back in balance.

"How are you doing, Chad? You always ask about me but you never mention how you're doing."

He took a sip of water, set his plate down and turned to me. "Thanks, Luna. I appreciate that. I'm good, though. I think I've finally gotten over my last breakup and I'm not sad about it anymore. My parents are getting along better, too."

The last sentence took me by surprise. I knew they had fights, more than most parents, but didn't know it had gotten worse. "You know you can talk to me anytime."

Chad smiled, "I do, even at one in the morning."

We both laughed but it was true. That was the kind of friendship we had. Even if I ended up moving away and we didn't see each other for months or years, we could still pick up where we left off and laugh about anything.

Bear came running into the living room just as a loud noise came from the kitchen. Chad and I both stood up holding our plates. We didn't know what had just happened, but based on the yelling coming from the other room, Bear had done something he shouldn't have. We both followed the voices from the kitchen.

"What happened?" I asked.

"Bear almost knocked over the whole cake," Mom replied.

"Well, he did knock over my piece and the dish shattered," said dad.

I saw that they were still cleaning up the remnants of the cake and dish and decided to help. I moved the cake to a safer place and wiped up the counter top. Dad put the broken pieces of glass into the trash and mom wiped up the floor.

"There, good as new," dad said.

"Well, it's been another long day. I'm going upstairs," I said. "Thanks for coming, Chad. Goodnight, everyone." I turned and went up to my room. I wasn't exactly tired enough to go to sleep, but I did want to be alone.

I went to my laptop and texted my friends. I was excited to see them tomorrow and discuss our summer trip. We kept sending each other things to look up and I told them to look up Club Med in Cancun. Any trip we took was going to be exciting, I couldn't wait.

We talked about Jenny starting her job on Monday. Trish's mom got another great check up from the doctor. Nancy was still checking out apartments in Pittsburgh. I shut my computer. Everyone was moving on with their lives and I was here doing nothing without any prospects. I felt like I was just wasting time.

I didn't want to feel sorry for myself, but I was feeling a bit depressed. I just needed to be more patient, that's all. I decided to turn on the tv. I flipped through all of the channels about three times until I left it on an old rerun of a favorite sitcom. I heard talking and laughing but I couldn't focus. I tried to get into it, but I just couldn't. I took my shower and climbed into bed. Bear jumped on my bed and curled up by my feet.

Today was another long day and I was glad it was over. Were all days going to feel like this? Tomorrow I would be hanging out with my friends and it should be more fun. We decided to make our lunch date at the beach. We were all going to bring something and enjoy the sun and sand. What better place to discuss a Mexican vacation?

I sat up and pet Bear. He was so soft and warm, without a care in the world. It was comforting for me, too, to have him here sleeping on my bed. It reminded me of when I was younger, when life was much simpler. I still remembered the day I got Bear. I looked up at the photo on my mirror. Dad was always surprising me, just like tonight.

Chapter 5

Today I woke up to a notification on my phone. My appointment to get my passport was in one hour. I suddenly remembered that I still needed my birth certificate. I jumped out of bed and ran downstairs, nothing. No note, no mother and no birth certificate. She forgot.

I dialed mom's number and it went to voicemail. I left a message asking her to tell me where it was. I would look for it. She called me back just as I was getting dressed and she said that she was sorry but she would look when she got home. Home? I needed it now!

I was so upset! How could she do this to me? She knew I needed it because I've been asking her every day for it. I took a chance and called dad. He didn't know where it was, either. There was no use trying to search the house, it might not even be here. For all I knew, it could be in a safe deposit box in some random bank. All I could do was change my appointment for next week. It was not a good way to start my day.

I ate a quick breakfast and then made sandwiches to take to the beach for lunch. With my calendar suddenly clear, I decided to go early and get us a good spot. I grabbed some drinks, blanket and towel and then went to change into my bathing suit.

On the car ride to the beaches on Presque Isle, I started wondering if this was going to be the last time I came here. If I got my acceptance letter today, I could be moving in with Nancy tomorrow. I was feeling nostalgic for things that haven't even happened, yet. I rolled down the windows and blasted the radio.

As I got closer to the beach, I decided to treat myself to a vanilla and orange sherbet twist cone at Sara's. It was iconic and if this was the last time I got to eat it, I would savor every lick. I pulled into beach ten and laid my blanket out. With everything ready, all I needed to do was wait for my friends to come.

It was about an hour later when the first text messages came through saying they were here. I waved and they came and brought more snacks and drinks. The four of us sat and discussed our vacation plans. We were all still open for suggestions, but Florida and California were quickly vetoed because Jenny wanted to go somewhere that required a passport.

Passports were a touchy subject for me, but I was going to assume I would eventually get one and it would come in time for this vacation. After nearly an hour of discussing pros and cons of various locations in Mexico and the Caribbean, we all agreed on Club Med Cancun. That was done. Now we had to decide on the exact week we would plan the trip. I had the whole summer open, as far as I knew, but the rest of them had to factor in their own schedules.

We were nearing the end of May, so we planned the trip for early August. That should be plenty of time for Trish and I to get our passports. With those details out of the way, we could finally enjoy the beach. I let the sound of the water and the warmth of the sun calm my thoughts.

I used to come to these beaches all the time with my family. I even came alone as soon as I had my license. I would miss the beaches the most if I have to move to Pittsburgh. The lake was beautiful but nothing compared to the sunsets in the evening. That was when the lake came to life. The shades of reds and oranges danced on the water until the sun was no longer visible. Even then, there were still remnants until the darkness took over completely.

We spent the next few hours just lounging, eating and talking. It was so therapeutic to all get together. We never knew when the next time would be when all four of us could set aside a whole afternoon, again. At three o'clock, we started to pack up. I didn't tell them I had dinner plans because I didn't want to feed into their conspiracy theories about me and Chad.

We hugged each other and knew this time together would be limited in the future. "I love you guys," I said, looking at each of them.

At home, I showered and changed. I heard mom come home and ran downstairs.

"Mom! I need that birth certificate," I yelled. "You made me miss my appointment today because I didn't have it."

"Okay, okay, I'll go look for it now."

I took Bear for a quick walk in order to calm down. I didn't mean to yell at mom just as she got home from work, but she has to know this is important to me. I walked around the block a couple of times and returned home. Mom was standing in the kitchen waiting for me.

"Get this back to me as soon as you're done with it," She said.

"I will." I took it upstairs and laid it on my desk with all the paperwork for my passport. I would finally be able to make my next appointment. It was nearly time to meet Chad, so I went outside to sit on the porch.

The evening breeze was still cool, so I went back in to grab my jacket. Chad was walking towards his car when I came back out and I waved. I sat in the passenger seat and he asked where we were going. It was my choice.

"I really don't care," I answered. "Wherever you want to go is fine for me."

Chad rolled his eyes. "I knew you were going to say that, so I made reservations at the bar and grill on the bay."

He gave me a sideways look and put the car in drive. I smiled and sat back into the seat. The earth and moon were in sync. We didn't talk much on the drive towards the water, there wasn't need. He played a classical music station on the radio and I let myself relax.

At the restaurant, he went up to the hostess and said, "Chad Parker, party of two." The hostess batted her eye lashes a few too many times and I just smiled. Even on a 'date' he was still getting hit on. He pulled out my chair and ordered a bottle of a local white wine. I was getting the full effect of what it must be like on a real date with Chad and it was pretty intimidating.

"So, how was the beach with the girls?" He asked.

I took a sip of wine and smiled. "It was wonderful. No doctor in the world could prescribe better medicine than an afternoon with my friends!"

This time he smiled. "I'm glad, you deserve it."

We ordered our food and sipped more wine. "How are your parents doing?" I asked.

Chad set his glass down and leaned back in his chair. This was not an easy subject for him to talk about, but he wouldn't sugar coat it for me, either. "Mom kicked dad out. We'll see how long it lasts," he said matter-of-factly.

I must have looked stunned. "It's okay. They do this all the time. I really should just get my own place so I don't have to see it, but part of me feels like I need to be there, you know?" Chad continued, "I could have left home a long time ago, almost did, but I feel like..." Chad's voice trailed off.

"You can't protect her your whole life, Chad," I said. Something I had been wondering for a long time finally came into focus. "This is why you've been sabotaging all of your relationships! As soon as a girl wants to get serious and talk about moving in together, you break up." It all made sense now, why this handsome guy couldn't keep a girlfriend.

Chad was quiet.

"I'm sorry, I didn't mean for it to come out like that," I said.

"But it's the truth," he replied, softly. "I know I can't keep living like this, though."

This boy that I've known my whole life had been hurting more than anyone else I knew. How did I not know it was this bad?

"Just promise me that you don't break up with the next girl that comes along because of this," I said.

"I promise," he said and then smiled.

We ate in comfortable silence until we finished our meal. I had the grilled salmon and he ordered the steak. It was delicious and I enjoyed myself more than I thought I would. I think he did, too. He was finally able to unburden himself with what had been troubling him and that kind of honesty felt good.

He paid the bill and we went out to his car. "Okay, my little moonbeam, where to for dessert?" He asked.

I laughed at his use of the childhood nickname he gave me so long ago. "Oh, I'd better not. I'm so full already."

"How about a soft serve at Sara's?"

"I'd better not have two in one day."

"Two?" He asked.

"I was here earlier remember?" I replied. "You can't drive past Sara's without getting a twist cone!"

We both laughed as we got in his car. We both passed on dessert and he drove us home. It was getting chilly and he turned on the heater. I couldn't remember the last time I ever felt so safe. There was no other way to describe it, other than gravity.

"Thank you for tonight, Chad. I had a really great time," I said.

"It was all for you. And I promise, it's the last time you will be center of attention, at least from me," he replied.

We hugged and went back to our own houses. Bear was at the door to greet me and I let him out quickly before coming in and locking the door. What a great day! Maybe I am in line to get some good luck. That would be great, actually, because I was still waiting to hear back from a couple places and good news would be very welcome.

Mom and dad were in bed, but I heard Alice still up. "Hey, how's it going?" I asked.

"Good," Alice replied. "Where've you been?"

"Out," I said. "Now I'm in."

Alice rolled her eyes and went back to her video game. I closed her door and entered my room. I flopped on my bed and looked up at the ceiling. Bear didn't want to be left behind and joined me on my bed. I sat up, kicked off my shoes and took off my jacket.

Again, I was blindly flipping through channels when I found a movie I liked. I showered, changed and curled up in bed with Bear. This was the perfect way to end the perfect day. I wasn't going to think any more about genetics, masters program or boys. It was just me and Bear watching a movie.

There was a very light tapping on my door. Alice poked her head in. "Can I borrow a dress?" She asked.

"Sure," I replied. "Which one?"

"The green one, Evan is taking me somewhere new tomorrow night and I want to wear something he hasn't seen, yet."

"Who were you out with anyway?" Alice asks from my closet.

I was about to say, 'none of your business' but decided to be honest, "Chad."

Alice stepped out of my closet. "Are you serious? I knew there was something between you guys."

"No, there isn't! We are just friends." I protested.

"That's what they all say."

"Alice, are you done, yet?" I asked, annoyed.

Alice walked out of my room slowly, holding my green dress, smiling at me the whole time. I threw my slippers at my door as she closed it just in time. Down the hall I could hear her laughing.

"Little sisters! Am I right, Bear?" I scratched Bear behind the ears and he rolled on his back. If only I had another dog instead of a sister, life would be perfect.

Chapter 6

As the days passed, I was beginning to feel lost. I wasn't sure where I belonged right now. I didn't like just sitting at home, although the relaxed time schedule was a nice change of pace, I wanted to be doing something. I thought about getting a little part-time summer job, like Alice. I could go back to work at Waldameer Amusement Park, why not?

I know, because I don't want to move backwards, I need to keep going forwards or else I will be permanently lost. I knew in my head this was temporary. I would eventually hear back from the school, I would eventually get my passport and make vacation plans and I would even get the genetic test results, eventually.

In the meantime, I must make the best of it. I was lucky because my parents weren't even pressuring me to get a job or make a decision. They knew I had worked hard to get to this moment and they were giving me space and time. I guess I was the only one who was trying to put a time limit on things. Let me just enjoy this summer.

June brought warmer days and I enjoyed spending them at the beach. Most of my friends were now working and that left just me to find things to do. I even drove to Pittsburgh with Nancy to help her look at apartments. It was hard for me, not knowing if I was coming with her or not for sure. She was great, though. She kept saying, 'we' when referring to the different rooms, neighborhoods and cafés to study in. I tried to be encouraging and enthusiastic, but it was getting harder. I knew the drill, by now everyone should have gotten their acceptance letter, if they got in.

Nancy and I spent the day in Pittsburgh before heading home. The two and a half hour ride was nice, especially in June. Even Nancy, who had the best excuse to just chill out this summer, got a part-time job. She was working downtown at an antique store a few hours each day. I suppose it wouldn't hurt if I started looking for something part-time, too.

I met Trish on her day off. She said that any day could be a day off, she just needed to meet a client if she received a call. The housing market in the city wasn't very good right now, but when you go outside the city, it was booming. Trish kept busy representing the whole area of Erie County, where builders were focusing on. Homeowners could get more land for their money the further out they went.

"People nowadays want horses, cows, goats and chickens so they need more land for that kind of thing," Trish said. Farm animals weren't her idea of fun, so she didn't always agree with her client's tastes. "For me, I want to be near all the action," she added.

"I don't know, I would love to have more land. Not necessarily for animals, but maybe some fruit trees or a garden...that would be nice," I said.

Trish considered my response, "Yes, I could handle a garden, but you can do that in the city, too."

We finished our lunch at the Sloppy Duck Restaurant. They have a great selection of fish and we chose seats near the water. Lunch time wasn't as crowded as dinner, since they featured live music in the evening. The marina was busy today. So many people were taking out their boats on this sunny, warm day. I wished I could be one of them.

Trish got a call just as we were finishing our fish sandwiches. "Gotta run, sorry," she said.

"It's okay, you have places you need to be," I replied. "I've got the check."

We stood up, hugged and then she was gone. I was happy that her real estate career was working out so well for her. Her mother was improving and getting stronger. The cancer was gone and we all prayed that it stayed away. Now Trish could focus on herself and maybe even find a place of her own, although she may not be ready to leave her mother just yet.

I know Trish had a lot on her plate but you would never know it. She had great people skills and I was sure she would be a huge success selling real estate around here. Maybe, instead of finding a place for her, she could get a bigger house for the whole family. That would be amazing.

I spent the rest of the afternoon just driving around and running errands. I found this cute bookstore at the Liberty Plaza and bought a couple of books from a local author. Now that I had time to sit and read, I was excited to get started.

As I pulled into the driveway I spotted Chad mowing the front yard. I waved and went in to get Bear, who was at the door and ready for a walk. Now that everyone in the house, except me, were working most days, I needed to pay more attention to Bear's schedule. He hadn't been out since I left for my lunch with Trish and I felt guilty.

I walked around the block and Chad was just finishing his mowing. He sat on this front steps and drank some water. I went over to sit with him. Bear came over, licked his face and then laid down on the cool pavement in the shade.

"How was your day?" He asked.

"Oh, it was good," I replied. "Had lunch with Trish, ran some errands, bought some books at Werner's and then came home."

"Sounds exciting," Chad said with a smile.

"Sounds boring," I corrected.

We both laughed because he knew I had too much time on my hands. I was trying to fill my days and keep busy but with each passing day, it was getting harder and harder to do.

"Well, we could use a bank teller," Chad said after he took another drink of his water. "Another one is quitting in a couple of weeks. She's moving to Columbus."

I didn't answer right away. It wasn't the job I was waiting for, but I also didn't want to hurt his feelings. "I will keep that in mind," I replied.

Chad smirked as he took another drink. I wasn't sure if his mentioning the job opening was just to tease me or if he legitimately thought I might want it. Either way, I wanted to change the subject.

"You know I still dream about that salmon," I said, jokingly.

He laughed so suddenly and organically, I had to laugh with him. Things were so easy with Chad.

"Well, I hope you and the salmon will be very happy together," he finally replied. "But seriously, it was great food. If you want to do it again, I can look up somewhere else that has great salmon..." Chad had turned to look at me, waiting for my response.

"I don't want to take up all of your time." I replied.

He laughed, again. He gestured to his front yard with his right hand. "You can see what I do to fill my time."

This time, I laughed. "Okay, fine. I'll let you know." We stayed sitting on his front steps for what seemed like hours. It was probably only ten minutes, but time stood still for that moment. I could hear other lawn mowers in the distance, birds singing in the trees and cars driving down West 27th Street, but it was all white noise.

I could remember all of the times we sat on this very step and played tag, hide and seek or some other game where we had to touch the railing or be out. All the kids from the neighborhood would be included in the games and at the end of the day, Chad and I would be sitting right here.

Kids didn't ride their bikes to each other's houses anymore or roller skate down the sidewalk. They were in their rooms playing video games or getting rides to the mall or something else that I couldn't even imagine. I'd like to think that I would carry on the tradition of playing tag outside in the yard with my kids.

I stood up and walked back to my house with Bear in tow. We waved to each other and I went back inside. Bear was happy to drink some water and lie down again on the carpet. I grabbed a snack and went to sit on the couch. I must have dozed off watching the news because I woke up when I heard mom come home.

"Hi, Luna, how was your day?"

"It was good. How about yours?" I asked.

Mom had brought home some donuts and cookies from work. It was always a nice perk about working at a bakery. I opened the box and picked out a chocolate covered donut.

"It was busy," she said. "Lots of birthday, weddings and graduations this time of year."

She put a frozen pizza in the oven and turned to me. "Don't forget to give me back your birth certificate when you're done with it. I want to keep it safe," she said.

I finished my donut and went to wash my hands at the sink. "I won't. My appointment is in a couple of days, so I'll be done with it after that."

Mom seemed satisfied with my response. She started cleaning off the kitchen table and I helped. Dad came home just as the pizza was coming out of the oven. He gave us each a hug and we sat down to eat our pizza and a salad.

"So, I think we decided to go to Club Med in Cancun for our graduation trip," I said.

"Oh, that sounds fun!" Dad replied. "When is this?"

"Early August, we need to make sure we leave plenty of time to get our passports back in the mail," I said.

"Pack plenty of sunscreen, and a hat," Mom responded. "The sun is hotter down there. Your fair skin will burn on the first day if you're not careful."

It was true. I had a hard time tanning. The rest of the family had nice golden tans all summer, but I had to really work at it. "I will," I said.

I helped clean up the dinner dishes and load the dishwasher. Dad took a few cookies from the box on the counter and went into the living room to find a game on the television. It didn't matter what day of the week it was, he could always find some sort of sport to watch on tv. It was his talent.

Mom, on the other hand, would tuck into a chair in the corner and either read or crochet. She preferred the quiet to the cheers and yells of a football game on tv. I did, too. I guess I got that quiet soul from my mother instead of the need for entertainment from my dad.

"I'm going to go get the mail," I said to no one.

Bear saw me head for the door and automatically assumed he would be joining me. Why not? It was going to be a short walk, but he could come along. I bent down to connect his leash and we slipped outside into the moonlight.

People were still out walking and sitting on their front porches. I waved to the old lady across the street as I went to the mailbox. It seemed like the usual junk mail and flyers. I let Bear do his thing and then he, reluctantly, followed me back inside.

I had set the mail on the corner of the kitchen counter and was about to walk away when I saw my name. Ms. Luna Gabriella Delaney. It had to be about the master's program. My heart started racing and I thought it would jump right out of my chest. My palms were sweaty and I was more afraid than excited. I didn't even want to touch it.

I thought about calling Nancy, but then reconsidered. Let me open it first and see what it said. I had to talk myself into it. I looked for a knife and sliced the top of the envelope open. I was starting to hyperventilate as I read the words:

"Dear Ms. Delaney, we regret to inform you..."

My fists crumpled the paper as I read the sentence and walked straight to my room and shut the door.

Chapter 7

Nancy took the news better than I did. She expected it. She knew that everyone who got into the master's program was probably already informed. It was me who was in denial for so long. I was just being stupid. I held out hope for months waiting for this letter and it was all shattered in seconds. I wasn't good enough to get in.

My future used to have forks in the road, now it was a straight line. No more choices, no more options, I needed to find a job. No, not just a job, a career. What was I going to do? I never put much time or effort into looking for a marketing job here because I was planning to continue my education, maybe get a job in Pittsburgh or even another state.

The half crumpled letter was sitting on my desk. I could feel it staring at me, so I got up and threw it away. I had my appointment at the post office today for my passport, so I got dressed and went downstairs. The house was quiet, everyone was at work. I poured my coffee and took Bear outside.

As we walked, I actually felt lighter. I guess the pressure of waiting for the letter was gone now. I was no longer being weighed down by the uncertainty of my future. It was clear now. That, in some ways, was better. I could focus now. No more distractions from finding a great job, I could put all my energy into job hunting.

But first, Mexico.

I was still giving myself the summer off. Of course, that didn't mean I couldn't still look for jobs, I just didn't have to apply to any of them, yet. I would do that later. I haven't even opened my computer in days. I had already heard all the bad news I was waiting to hear. The rest could wait.

The post office was busy. I stood in line at the window designated for passports. I was right on time and had everything in a big yellow envelope.

"Luna Delaney?" A large older gentleman called out from behind the counter.

"Here!" I called out, as if he was asking for attendance at school.

He gestured for me to come forward, and by the look on his face, he wanted me to hurry. I handed him my envelope of documents, forms and payment. He checked everything, looked at my photographs and started stapling, stamping and shoving everything into the envelope. He handed me my original documents back, satisfied that the copies were accurate.

"You should have it back in six to eight weeks," the man said in monotone.

"Thank you," I replied and returned to my car.

That was easy. Now I could treat myself to a coffee at the nearby coffee shop. I ordered an iced coffee, sat down and pulled out my phone. I sent a text to my friends saying that my passport was in the mail. This was followed by numerous texts sharing their excitement for our Mexican vacation.

After checking my emails on my phone, I almost deleted one that I thought was junk. But it wasn't. It said my genetic test results were available on their website. Create a login to proceed. I put my phone down. Another thing I will get to when I opened my computer. I was in no hurry to see those results.

I decided to take a drive to the beach. I walked to the lake and put my feet in. The water was still chilly but it felt good on this warm June day. Families were starting to arrive and pull out their coolers for lunch. Some were heating up the charcoal grills on the beach for picnic lunches. The smells were making me feel nostalgic, but the crowds were making me feel more alone. I decided to go back home and finally open my computer.

I was secretly dreading it and found any excuse to delay the inevitable. I took Bear for another walk and this time we stayed out for an hour. I made a sandwich and went up to my room. I couldn't put it off any longer.

Before I opened the email from the genetics lab, I browsed my other emails. There was an email from Chad forwarding me the bank teller opening at his bank. As much fun as it would be to work with Chad, I decided to not apply for that one. I was still holding out hope for a real job in marketing.

There was an email from the school I didn't get in. Delete. Trish had sent us all an email showing us the resort we wanted to book. We were to look it over and make sure it was what we wanted. I clicked on the link and immediately fell in love. Image after image of people lounging in the sun with drinks in their hands. I replied back with my vote.

Jenny sent us all an email inviting us to go wine tasting in North East, PA. I checked the date, it was for tomorrow. I quickly replied with a big 'YES' and hoped I wasn't too late. I immediately got a text back from Jenny saying, 'finally responding' and an eye roll emoji. She said she knew I would want to go and was already included in the count and that details are in the email.

I actually got side tracked and started looking at jobs. I was feeling anxious and wanted to know what was out there. There were a few that actually sounded promising and decided to fill out a few applications. Why not? Nothing may ever come from it, but at least I can say I tried. I was scrolling through endless job listings and feeling more and more discouraged. Some wanted to pay as little as possible, others wanted a master's degree and then most wanted experience.

I eventually made it back onto the genetic testing kit's email. I clicked on the link and created an account. It took awhile to navigate the website and eventually found my test results. There was a lot of medical jargon that I didn't understand but when I clicked on the little tab, it gave a more detailed description of that particular test.

I never knew there were so many genes that could be tested! There was everything from genetic traits, such as hair color and whether you preferred sweet or sour foods, to letting you know if you are predisposed to various diseases. I had fun looking at all of the traits and found out that they were pretty accurate.

It was actually pretty interesting. I texted Trish to let her know I finally took the test and got my results back. She sent me a thumbs up emoji and asked if there were any 'surprises'. I let her know that so far things were looking good. I was seeing a lot of test results with a 'negative' response, so that was probably a very good thing.

My phone told me I had another text and stopped to read it. It was from Chad. He wanted to know if I had seen the email he sent about the job opening. I told him I did and thanked him for thinking of me. I also let him know I didn't get into the master's program, so I was going to keep looking for jobs. He said he was sorry and that things will work out.

They had better work out. I was tired of this limbo of not knowing what to do. Another text came through. This time from Trish, again. She wanted to know if I had checked out the ancestry feature of the website, yet. She said she enjoyed tracing her family tree and maybe visit Germany someday to continue the search. I told her I would.

I found the tab that initiated the dna search for my genetic links. I zoomed in on the United States and could see some family around Pennsylvania and the tri-state area. I don't think anyone else in my family took this kind of test because they weren't showing up. I clicked on a few people who showed up as third cousin or fourth cousin. This wasn't that interesting.

Just as I was getting ready to log out, the map expanded. That's when I found my surprise. I had genetic links in Italy! My parents never said anything about having Italian ancestors. I was expecting to see more fourth or fifth cousins, but when I zoomed in on the two little dots near Rome I nearly fainted. That couldn't be right.

I stood up and slammed my laptop shut. What did I just see? There was no way! I paced the room and Bear watched me walk in circles. This has to be a mistake. My dna sample got mixed up with someone else. It just wasn't possible.

I took some more deep breaths and sat back down on the chair. I tried to keep my heart rate and breathing as close to normal as possible so I closed my eyes. I was so close to texting Trish and saying her genetic test kit was a bunch of garbage, but I was curious and decided that I'd better double check.

I slowly opened my eyes and scrolled back to Italy. There was no mistaking the words this time. 'Paternal match, C.D.V. Potential half-sibling match, Marco'. Who were C.D.V. and Marco? It didn't make any sense. Paternal match? My father is right now at work in an insurance agency in Erie, PA, not in a small town outside of Rome, Italy. Sibling match? I don't have a brother named Marco.

What was this website trying to tell me? I had so many questions. I'm sure this wasn't what Trish meant by 'surprises' but I sure was being surprised! I even got my dictionary out to look up the word paternal. Surely there was another obscure definition that didn't mean father. Nope.

Well, I wasn't going to tell anyone about this. It was most certainly a mistake and I wasn't going to be the reason everyone had a good laugh. I closed my laptop and stood up. I wanted to put as much distance between me and that lying piece of electronics that I could.

I still felt anxious and shaken, though. Who were they to question who my father was? I was pretty sure if there was something going on, my mother would have told me.

I paced my room, again. Bear's eyes followed me, just in case I decided to leave the room and take him for a walk. Otherwise, he stayed laying on my bed, oblivious to the hurricane of emotions running through my body right now.

I realized I still had my birth certificate in my purse and pulled it out. It had a big crease in it and mom probably would get mad, so I laid it on my desk to smooth it out. As I was rubbing my hands from top to bottom, I start reading all of the entries. I had never seen the document before, only checking for the name to make sure it was mine before taking it to the post office.

Date of birth, January 23rd. Hair, brown. Eyes, brown. Weight, six pounds. Length, 27 inches. Mother's maiden name, Shirley Grant. Father's name: Cosimo Dante Vernetti.

That was the moment I fainted.

Chapter 8

I left my folded birth certificate on the kitchen counter for mom and left the house. It was Saturday and I was meeting my friends for our wine tasting tour. I still haven't mentally recovered from the information I learned last night. C.D.V. Cosimo Dante Vernetti. I had never heard that name before in my life. Now I couldn't get it out of my head. Cosimo. Who was that?

I didn't even remember how I got to Jenny's house. She had a shiny new red SUV, so we all climbed inside. Jenny didn't drink much, so she was okay to drive. It was time with my friends that I really needed right now. Wine, too, maybe.

They were talking amongst themselves about various topics. I tried to pay attention, but I couldn't. I leaned my head on the window and closed my eyes. I wasn't sleeping, there was no way I could feel that calm. My head was spinning. I debated whether to confront my mother about the information. The birth certificate confirmed it. She had to have known that I would see that, at least.

Maybe she was waiting for me to say something. What do I say? How could my dad not be my dad? He's the only father I knew and could even remember. Did this have something to do with why they didn't get married before I was born? Was she in Italy at the time? I had so many questions.

"Luna!"

I opened my eyes to see all three of them staring at me. "I'm sorry. What?"

"We were wondering if you started packing, yet?" Nancy asked.

I smiled and tried to clear my head. "No, have you guys started?"

"Of course!" Trish replied. "This is going to be epic, so I had to start shopping and packing now."

We reached the first winery and we had our tasting glasses in front of us. Everyone was still looking at me. I tried to act natural, but it wasn't working.

"What's wrong?" Jenny asked. "You haven't been yourself since you got in the car."

I didn't dare say anything about my family tree. "I got the letter from the school," I said. "I didn't get in."

My friends spent the rest of the afternoon trying to console me and cheer me up. They thought this was the news that had me so down and distracted. It was, until I got even worse news. I just wasn't ready to talk about the rest, yet. There were other people I needed to talk to first.

I tried to enjoy the day. I loved hearing their stories and spending time with my friends. I would tell them eventually but I needed to process it first. I sipped wine, ate crackers and cheese and commented on the fruitiness or the dryness of each one. It was a welcome distraction that I tried to allow.

I bought a few bottles along the way. By the end of the afternoon, we visited three vineyards and I actually started enjoying myself. By the third one, though, we were all tipsy and I had almost let down my guard and told them, almost.

My head was feeling clearer by the time I got home and saw Chad painting his porch swing. I walked over to him and sat on the steps.

"Where have you been?" He asked.

"Drinking some wine." I showed him the box of wine I brought back.

"I see," Chad replied. He set down his paint brush and joined me on the steps. "Are you feeling okay?"

"Yes, I'm feeling much better, thank you."

Chad laughed and my answer. We sat for a moment not saying anything. The earth and moon didn't always need words. Then I blurted it out.

"I don't think my dad is my dad."

Chad just looked at me. I think he was waiting for me to elaborate but I didn't, so the sentence just hung there for a long time.

"Why do you think that?" He finally asked.

"Well, two reasons. First, there is another man listed on my birth certificate as my father. Second, I did the genetic test kit from Trish and a paternal match showed up in Italy."

Again, there was silence. I looked over at Chad and his eyebrows were bunched together like he was concentrating on something really hard. I could tell he was trying to process this new information.

"You should go meet him," he said matter-of-factly.

"Go and meet him?" I asked. My voice was too high pitched. "What am I going to say, 'Hi, I'm your daughter?' What if he doesn't know about me?"

"Did you ask your mother about him? Maybe she can give you some answers."

"Or lies," I replied. "She obviously didn't want to tell me or she would have already. What if my dad doesn't know?"

"Listen, I just know that if it was me, I would want to meet him. It doesn't have to change anything. Even if your mom tells you everything or nothing, the fact is your father is still in Italy. It might be too late or it might not be, but you won't know until you see him."

"And I have a half-brother."

Chad ran his hand through his blond hair. It was getting longer and it stayed ruffled. He just shook his head and said quietly, "You should go."

This was too much to think about. I wasn't expecting that response from Chad, but it made sense. Even if I talked to my mother, how do I know she would tell me the truth now. I could confront her when I got back from Italy, if I went.

Chad put his arm around me. "I wish I could help you with this. I would go with you if I could, but this is probably something you need to do alone. But, I could use an Italian vacation…"

I leaned my head on his shoulder. The gravitational pull was strong. "I'll let you know what I decide." I stood up and stretched. "Thanks for listening, though. You're the only person I've told."

He looked surprised to hear that. I guess he assumed I would have told my friends today. "I'm only a house, a phone call and a text away."

I waved goodnight and returned home. My mother must have taken my birth certificate back to its hiding place because it was no longer on the counter top. Maybe she will bring it up. I doubted it, though. She probably thinks I didn't even notice that there was a different man listed as my father.

Dad. I heard a baseball game on and walked to the living room. Dad was sitting on the couch eating potato chips. I suddenly felt sorry for him. Raising another man's daughter had to be hard. It was probably safe to assume that Alice is their biological child, my half-sister.

This was all beginning to get very complicated. And yet, it was starting to make more sense. The differences in our skin tones, hair and face. I had some features from my mom, but none from my dad. I tried desperately to look for some, but I never could find any similarities.

I grabbed a can of pop and joined him on the couch. "Who's winning?"

"Hey Luna! The Pirates are winning."

Dad and I sat on the couch eating chips and sipping our drinks watching the Pirates play some other team with a bird on their jersey. I didn't keep up with sports, but I enjoyed sitting with dad. He cheered when they made a hit or scored. I had so many questions for him, but they were better left unasked.

During a commercial I decided to tell him my news. "Hey dad, I didn't get in the master's program."

Dad put his arm around me and squeezed. "It's okay, my little moon, you'll find something soon that's even better than that stupid school."

His use of my childhood nickname made me tear up. Was I still his little moon? "Thanks, dad." I stood up and went to my room.

I sat at my desk and opened my laptop. I logged into the family tree and zoomed in to Italy again. This time I grabbed a notebook and pen. When I clicked on Cosimo's name, there was no information listed. He and Marco were both listed in the same town, Frascati, Italy. I clicked on Marco to get some more details. There wasn't any address or phone number listed, only an email.

Should I email him? Surely the son could speak some English, enough to communicate with me. I couldn't just come out and say, 'Hi, I'm your sister'. He probably doesn't know anything about it. Instead, I just wrote down his email and I would think about it later.

I pushed away from my desk. I had to think of a reason to email him so that he would definitely email back, with an address. This would take some time.

I flipped to a blank page in my notebook and decided to make a packing list for Mexico. Wait, if I go to Mexico, I won't have enough money to go to Italy, too. There was no way for me to hide a trip to Italy from my parents, unless they think I'm in Mexico! I hated the idea of missing the Mexican trip, but if I could time them perfectly, they would think I was in one place when I was really in another. If I went.

I still wasn't convinced that I should go to Italy. I couldn't just fly over, walk right up to Cosimo and introduce myself, unless he wanted me to. It was strange that he and his son were listed on the genetic testing website. Could this be their way of reaching out, confirming for me that he is, indeed, my father?

I felt like the Russian captain in the movie The Hunt for Red October. Was I a Russian defector testing to see if the enemies in the other submarine were friendly or not? If I respond to Cosimo saying I was his daughter, would he confirm it? One ping only, please.

My palms were sweating and I was feeling very anxious, again. I tried searching his name but there were too many hits. I couldn't make sense of most of them because they were in Italian.

I pulled out my phone. It was nine o'clock at night. I texted Chad, 'Are you up?'.

He texted back immediately, 'I'll be right over'.

I put on my robe and walked downstairs and out the front door. Chad was just walking across my yard when we sat on my front steps together.

"I'm scared, but I think I want to go," I said.

"I knew you would," he replied. "Do you want me to come with you?"

"No, you're right, I need to do this alone."

"Yes, but if you can't, I can just go for moral support." Chad nudged me with his shoulder. "I'm serious, I have time off, I would go with you if you can't do it alone."

"I know you would and you don't know how much I appreciate the offer, but if I go, I need to go alone."

"Okay."

Just the closeness of him was already calming me down. I focused on his breathing. I closed my eyes and took deep breaths. When I finally opened my eyes I saw that I was looking up at the sky.

"It's a full moon tonight," I said.

"That's good luck, you know," Chad replied.

"I hope so."

"It is, moonbeam, it is," he replied.

"Thank you, Chad."

"Anytime."

We stayed like that for several more minutes. I was sure he could hear my breathing slow down. Anyone else would think I was crazy, that I had screws loose in my head, but not Chad. I was there for him when his parents were fighting and he needed to sit on my porch for a few minutes. Earth and moon.

Chapter 9

The following week I had plans with my friends to meet up at the beach. This would be the perfect time to tell them that I wasn't going with them to Mexico. I had time to really think about it and I finally made my decision. I still hadn't said anything to my parents about what I found out. As far as they were concerned, I was heading to Mexico in six weeks.

I won't be, though. I'm not sure how my friends will take it, but I hope they will understand. They may not like that I've kept this from them, but I hoped they would understand that, too. I was feeling pretty nervous on the drive to the beach. I was dropping a huge bombshell on my friends and it wasn't going to be easy to say or hear.

I waited until we had all gone swimming and were now sun bathing on the sand to break the news. I was sure they could hear my heart pounding.

"So, I have some good and bad news," I said. All eyes were on me. I took a deep breath and continued. "I'm not going with you to Mexico."

At this news, they all sat up. "What?"

"I'm going to Italy." Silence.

"What do you mean you're going to Italy?" Jenny asked.

"Well, you remember that genetics kit that Trish gave all of us," I paused. They all nodded their heads. "Well, when I searched using the dna for a family tree, I got two hits, in Italy."

"How?" Trish asked.

All of their faces were blank. I could see I needed to give a full play by play of the last couple of weeks. I explained about finding just initials at first as a paternal match, then the birth certificate. I showed them a picture of it on my phone. They were all still speechless. I explained that I wanted to go meet him.

"But I can't afford two trips, so if I timed it so that you guys left for Mexico at the same time I left for Italy, then my parents would think I was with you. Are you in?"

"Sure, if that's what you really want," Nancy said.

"Yes, I do. I know I won't get the full story from my mother, even if she did decide to tell me about him. I have to go see him in person, too."

I felt relief that my friends finally knew. We discussed the plans in detail and they expressed a desire to come with me. "No, I've got to do this alone."

"Okay, fine, but when they accept you with open arms, we will fly over and see this new family of yours," Jenny replied.

I knew they meant well, but I already had a happy family here. I didn't know what I was expecting in Italy, but I was pretty sure they wouldn't just open their arm and welcome me. There was a reason that twenty-two years later, I was still a secret.

They were starting to accept the fact that I wasn't going with them on their vacation. The one thing we had been planning together since graduation. I was sad to be missing out, but this was also an opportunity I couldn't pass up. If I didn't go now, when would I have another chance like this? I didn't have a job, there was already a vacation in the works and I had the money.

The conversation was slowly steering away from disappointment to enthusiasm for my new adventure. I would have described it as more of a suicide mission, but hopefully things would go better than that. They were giving me ideas on how to get Marco to supply his address without being creepy or giving anything away.

I kept thinking that they were online for a reason. It had to be as a way to reach out to me. I knew nothing more than their names. Their physical descriptions were a complete mystery to me. I would be going in blind, other than the fact that Cosimo was somehow connected to a winery. We couldn't find out more than that.

He either worked at one or his family had one, it didn't matter. It was the man I wanted to see, not a winery. We had wineries here, if I've seen a few rows of grapes, I've seen them all. I just kept wondering what kind of man Cosimo was. Did he love my mom? How did they meet? I hoped that I would have the chance to ask him.

We all packed up and left the beach. It was getting late. I drove home and went right to my computer. Staring at the two little dots that represented my father and half-brother weren't going to give me any more answers.

Just then I heard a loud crash come from downstairs. I closed my laptop and ran down to see my mother standing in the kitchen surrounded by broken glass. Dad appeared from the living room and Alice came from the backyard.

"What happened?" Dad asked.

"I was filling the vase with water and I guess my hands were still wet. It just slipped right out of my hands." Mom was starting to cry.

Dad came over and lifted mom out of the wreckage and carried her into the living room. Alice and I cleaned up all of the broken glass. We swept and vacuumed until it was all gone. I was starting to get suspicious. Did mom really just lose her grip or was she starting to think that I knew the truth?

It was maddening how much I was overthinking everything. I knew it but couldn't help it, either. Did Alice suspect that I wasn't her full-blooded sister? Through it all, I still refused to discuss it with my family until after I returned from Italy. That way, I would have my own evidence in case she tried to make up a story.

I needed to clear my head. As soon as I reached for his leash, Bear was right by my feet wagging his little tail. I wanted to walk as far as I could, until I stopped thinking about all of this. I could probably walk all the way to Tampa and still not stop thinking about it.

We had been gone two hours. Bear and I had stopped for ice cream and then sat in the park for a bit. It was really refreshing to get out and have a change of scenery. I think Bear even made a girlfriend over on Cascade Street, but I couldn't be sure.

As we turned the corner onto our street, my heart dropped when I saw police cars. I pulled Bear into a run and was relieved to know it wasn't our house, but my heart stopped when I saw they were at Chad's. I stood on my front yard waiting to see who they were taking away.

Chad came running out his back door and stopped in front of me. "Wanna get out of here?"

He wasn't really waiting for an answer. He jumped in his car and started the engine. I had just enough time to put Bear in the house before we were taking off down the street. This was one of those times we didn't need words. I already knew it was bad, really bad.

I didn't know where he was going, but I knew we were heading for the lake. He took a right and I saw that he wanted to go to the public dock. He parked and we got out. He sat on the edge of the dock with his feet dangling over the edge.

"I wish I was going with you, Luna," Chad said softly.

"Come!" I was desperate to get his attention. "Come with me, I would love for you to come."

Chad kept his gaze on the water, feet swinging over the edge of the concrete dock. "I envy you, Luna. You're the strongest person I know. You're not afraid of anything."

"You're wrong, Chad," I replied. "I'm afraid of everything. I'm afraid I'm making a huge mistake by going. I'm afraid how this will effect my family. I'm afraid of what my future is going to be. I'm afraid of what you are going to do next."

"No, that's not fear, that's strength and courage because you will do it anyway. Whether you're afraid or not, you still keep going. I can't. I can't even move out of my house or maintain a relationship. I can't."

I was very worried about his frame of mind. What did he see today? What did he do? I have never seen him this shaken before. I was afraid for him. I came up behind him and gave him a hug. He leaned his head on my arm and I felt the wetness of his cheek. He was crying, silently. His hair smelled of pine and spice, he had just showered.

I came to sit down beside him. It was like coaxing a scared animal to trust you. "I'm going to get you out of there." They were just words, for now, and he knew it.

"Okay."

"I mean it. My full moon wish is for your happiness."

Chad finally looked at me. "I'm sorry. I didn't mean to drag you into this."

"That's what I'm here for," I replied. "Do you want to talk about it?"

He let out a long, deep breath. "It's the same story, different day. I got in between them and he hit me, a full on punch to my face."

I couldn't hide my shock. I drew in a breath and turned his face further to the right. Sure enough, a black eye was forming, fast.

"I didn't hit him back. I wanted to, but I didn't. Mom called the cops and I bolted out the back. That's when you saw me."

I walked to the little cafe on the dock and asked for a bag of ice. I gave it to Chad to help with the swelling. He winced but kept it there as best he could. We sat and watched the sunset. How did life get so complicated? I wanted to protect him, but that wasn't what he needed. He needed a friend.

"Come stay at my place tonight. Let things cool off at your house," I offered.

"Thanks, maybe."

"It'll be like the old days, our slumber parties and forts," I replied. I tried to be light-hearted but it was a very heavy situation. I wasn't even sure if the cops were waiting to question him when we got back. I didn't want to push too hard, we were on his time frame right now.

As the sun set, it started to get a little chilly. I shivered and he offered to go back into the car. Chad started the engine and turned on the heater for me. Then he took my hand.

"Thank you, Luna, I mean it. I don't know what I'd do without you." Then he kissed my hand and let it go.

He put the car in gear and we drove home. I knew he was eager to get back, so was I. I didn't know what to expect. Would there be more cops or would they be all gone. As we turned the corner to our street, I was relieved to see a nice quiet neighborhood. If I didn't know any better, I would think it was perfect.

He pulled into his driveway and we sat in silence. Still in our own little bubble, no distractions from the outside world. It was dark, so I couldn't see his face but all of a sudden he got out of the car, came around and opened my door. As I stood up, he hugged me.

When he finally released me I saw the black eye getting darker. The street lights reflected off the wetness of his cheeks, more silent tears. My heart was breaking. He turned and walked back into his house.

Chapter 10

Over the next few days, my plans were in motion. Then days turned into weeks. My family was still thinking I was going to Mexico when I was secretly going to Italy. I had been in constant touch with Chad and he assured me he was fine. His father hadn't been home since that night and things were calming down at his house. I prayed that was the truth.

I had to keep up the charade of going to Mexico by leaving a Spanish language book laying around the house or a brochure of Club Med Cancun in the kitchen. Secretly, I had my tour book of Rome and a map of Frascati, Italy. I had my packing list for my trip, but also another one for a decoy. It was getting chaotic, but it was also exciting.

One day I saw Alice coming out of my room and I got very defensive. "What are you doing in there?"

She paused and then showed me the denim skirt she was borrowing. She gave me a mean side eye and kept walking into her room. I had to be very careful not to leave anything out for anyone to see. Mom came in here to get laundry and dirty towels. Dad didn't usually come in, but he did pop his head in when it was time for dinner. Alice was always in here.

I didn't think my sister would say anything or even care what I was doing, but if she were to mention anything to my parents, they would definitely get suspicious. It was hard not saying anything to them. I was never one to keep secrets, especially one as big as this. I just hoped that when I finally did tell them what I did, they weren't furious that I lied for so long. I had been lying, literally, the entire summer. Now I was feeling guilty, again.

I just felt that the only way I could get an honest answer was if I investigated by myself first. They may see it as going behind their backs, but I just wanted the truth. Surely they would see that, too. I need to know where I came from and who I came from.

It was the end of June, so my friends and I finalized our dates and bought our plane tickets. We were all leaving August fourth, they were heading south and I was going east. I was trying to find the most reasonable place to stay in Rome. I didn't want a hostel, hotels were too expensive, so I decided to do an apartment rental. I could save money by having a kitchen, too.

I was feeling warm and wanted to go outside. Bear met me at the door and I took him out with me. I was surprised to see Chad out washing his car. I hadn't really seen him much the last couple of weeks.

"Hey, stranger," I said.

He smiled and turned the hose in my direction. I screamed and Bear tried to catch the water. He turned the water off and came over to me.

"Where are you headed?" He asked.

"Oh, just the usual walk around the block."

"Do you want company?"

"Sure!"

Chad walked with us as we went up one street and over the other. At first he didn't talk and I didn't pressure him. I knew he'd tell me anything when he was ready.

"I'm sorry about that night," he said.

"You never have to apologize," I replied.

"I scared you and I never wanted that to happen."

Yes, he did scare me, but I understood the situation, most of it. "How are things now?"

"Well, he's been back a few times."

I didn't ask what that meant. "How's work?"

"Work is good. We hired a new teller. She's kind of cute."

I smiled. I was sure she thought the same thing of him. I tripped on a crack in the sidewalk and Chad caught my elbow. Then he took Bear's leash from me so I could steady myself. "My friends and I are going to the dock for fireworks on the fourth of July, do you want to come with us?"

"Sure," he replied.

I wasn't sure how solid his commitment was to our plans, but at least he didn't say, 'no'. I would follow up with him in a few days to see where his head was at. We were coming back towards our houses and he asked how my plans for Italy were coming along.

"Good, I think I know where I'm going to stay, I just need to book it soon," I replied. "Do you think you could drop me off at the airport, and pick me up the following week? I mean, I can get a ride from someone else if..."

"No, I will," he interrupted. "I want to be there when you go and then hear all about it when you come back home."

"Okay, thanks."

When we arrived back at my house, we waved goodbye and I went inside.

TONIGHT WAS THE FIREWORKS on the dock. I was so excited to see everyone. Even Chad confirmed he would be coming and I would ride with him. I got my passport in the mail yesterday, so I was ready for my trip to Italy. So far, news had not leaked out to my family, either. I was feeling good about going and I just hoped that I came home with answers.

I really only had one more major thing to do before my trip and that was to book my apartment rental. I found the one I liked best which was right near Roma Termini station. I would take the train from the airport to that station and walk only a block to my rental.

The owner's name was Antonio Rossi and I emailed him my details and paid online. In theory, things should move smoothly from there. I was now just waiting confirmation and instructions on how to get into the apartment. I looked up the location online and could see that there was a restaurant right next door. Perfect.

I wrote it all down in my notebook and hid it in my desk. I have come too far to get caught now. My checklist was getting smaller, too. Only a few more things to pick up and I would be ready.

Chad texted that he was outside. I was in a great mood and couldn't wait to see my friends. It felt like weeks since I had seen everyone last. As we drove towards downtown, I couldn't help but make sure he really wanted to go.

He laughed, "Yes, I wouldn't be going if I didn't want to."

"Just making sure," I replied.

I was getting more and more excited the closer we got to the dock. As soon as I saw my friends, I ran and we all jumped into a big group hug. Chad just rolled his eyes as we screamed and jumped in a circle.

I looked over at him. "Aw, feeling left out?"

Right on cue, Nancy, Trish and Jenny all ran over to include him in their group hug. All he could do was accept it, point a finger at me and mouth the words, 'I'll get you'. It was already starting out to be a great night!

We all sat down and waited for the fireworks to start. Chad was actually having fun and laughing with the girls. I think he had a little crush on Jenny, but I also think Jenny met someone. She hadn't officially said anything to us about him, but I've noticed a few posts of hers on social media had a mystery guy in them.

We had found a grassy spot, away from the crowds and we laid back on the ground. This was exactly what I thought about when I imagine hanging out with my friends. We were all laying side by side and still talking and giggling, just like when we were younger. Even Chad and I used to lay on the front yard and look for cloud animals.

He took my hand and I looked at him. This time he mouthed, 'thank you'. I squeezed his hand and released it. We all jumped when the first fireworks fizzled and popped in the sky. There were red, blue and green ones. The light from the sky reflected in our faces. It was a magical night.

The fireworks reflected on the water, too. They were dancing on the waves and ripples. I wanted to remember this forever. We were all going on our separate journeys in a month. The outcome of mine could change things forever. I was taking a leap of faith that it would all be okay either way.

On the way home we talked about the night. There had been street vendors, so we had found something to eat. The fireworks even seemed more grand this year. Maybe it was just that I was open to all possibilities lately and it seemed bigger than it was. I don't know. Maybe I'm just overthinking, again.

Chad shifted in his seat and looked like he had something on his mind. "Just say it," I encouraged.

I had taken him by surprise because his eyebrows shot up and he turned to me, "What?"

"I know there is something you want to either say or ask, so just say it."

He looked even more uncomfortable that he was put on the spot. "Um, okay," he started. "Can I stay with you tonight?"

He had said it so quietly that if there was music playing I would never have heard him. "Of course," I answered. I never questioned him further or asked for a reason. That was our unspoken language. If you need help, just ask, no need to explain.

We were silent the rest of the way. I saw him physically relax as we got closer to home. I hated that he wrestled with his demons the whole night. If he would have asked at the beginning, he probably would have had more fun. Was he pretending all night? I didn't think so, I think he has a great way of compartmentalizing his emotions.

He pulled into his driveway but walked to my house. He already had a bag packed in the trunk. I didn't ask about it, just opened the door and let him in.

"Do you want a beer?"

"Only if you're having one," he replied.

"I am." I took two bottles of beer out of the fridge and we sat on the living room couch. It was nearly midnight, so everyone was either asleep or close to it. We propped our feet up and sipped our beers.

"Thank you for this," he said.

"For the beer?"

Chad rolled his eyes. "For all of this," he gestured to the whole room with his left hand.

I knew what he meant. "No need to thank me."

I took the empty bottles to the kitchen and we went upstairs. I had a very fuzzy rug beside my bed that he always slept on when he stayed overnight as kids. Tonight that was where he slept. I gave him a few blankets and he curled up with my extra pillow.

I went to the bathroom and brushed my teeth. It had been a long day and I was exhausted. When I came back I thought he was already asleep, his breathing was so steady. I tried to be quiet as I got into bed and turned off the light. I plugged my phone in to charge and laid down.

A few minutes later I heard Chad say very quietly, "Goodnight, little moon."

"Goodnight, earth," I whispered and went to sleep.

Chapter 11

Over the next few weeks leading up to my trip to Italy, I had a lot of time to think. Too much time. Every time I walked into the living room I saw the family portraits full of smiling faces. Were they all happy? I realized the earliest family photos with my dad in them were when I was one or two years old.

What happened right before and after I was born? I may never know the real answers to all of my questions, but I was sure going to try to find out. I was putting a lot of hope into this trip and I would be devastated if I didn't get any answers from it.

I was sitting on the couch turning pages in an old photo album. I smiled at pictures taken at my third birthday when dad came in and joined me on the couch. He had a beer and grabbed the remote control.

"Are you going to watch the game with me?" He asked.

"Dad, you know I'm not a big sports fan."

He laughed. "One of these days you will surprise your old man. You take after me in so many other outdoor activities, why not sports?"

Now it was me who was laughing. "Oh, you mean like hunting and fishing?" I hated both. Well, maybe hate was too strong of a word, but I did not enjoy them like he did.

"Exactly!" We both enjoyed the lighthearted banter, but for me, it was just another reminder that he wasn't my biological father. He continued to scroll through the channels until he found a baseball game.

I kept looking at old photographs. It wasn't until I was six that I saw my mom pregnant in the pictures. I had never really thought about that much. Who thinks about an age gap between siblings and suspects that there were different fathers? I supposed that back then it was easier to get away with, kids weren't going to ask questions.

Watching my father cheer on the teams made me want to believe that we were a big happy family. It didn't really matter where I came from or from whom. I was loved, that I knew for sure. I stood up, gave my dad a kiss on his cheek and went up to my room.

I still had to let Marco know I was coming. It was strange thinking that I was emailing my potential half-brother about a casual visit, but I didn't want him to know, at least not yet. My friends and I had been brainstorming different scenarios and I think we came up with a good enough cover story to get in.

I opened my laptop and went to my email. I shook out my hands and took a deep breath before beginning. We had decided that since they liked wine, that was going to be my way in.

"Dear Mr. Marco Vernetti,

My name is Gabriella Delaney (I decided to use my middle name, just in case he knew my first name) and I represent a vineyard in Pennsylvania. Our winery is young and promising but I am reaching out to various wine connoisseurs throughout your region to get personalized feedback regarding our latest vintage.

I will be in Italy in August and more specifically, the region of Frascati on August eighth. Please send me your address so that I may have our wine delivered ahead of my arrival. Also, provide me with a time to come and meet with you and Mr. Cosimo Dante Vernetti on this day.

Best Regards,

Gabriella Delaney"

Besides the fact that the vineyard was fake, I also had Nancy design a wine label to match the new bogus winery and we attached it to the bottles I got from the wine tasting. I attached a few photos of the doctored bottles and waited for an answer.

The waiting was agonizing. What if they said, 'No, thank you'. That could be the end of it. I was sure that once I arrived in Italy, someone could do more digging and find an address for Cosimo, but I didn't want to just show up. At least this way I was invited, sort of.

I looked at the time and figured that with the time difference, they would not be waking up for a few more hours and probably wouldn't respond right away anyway. I had time to kill. It was late and I wasn't sleepy. I decided to take Bear for a walk.

It was late July and the night air was still warm. It felt wonderful. I didn't go far, just up and down my street. I noticed Chad's light on and decided to send him a text.

'Are you up?' I texted.

He immediately responded, 'Where are you?'

'Outside.'

It didn't take long for him to appear at his doorway. Bear and I walked over and sat on his front steps. "So, how are things going?"

"Good."

"That's good." There wasn't any more explanation.

"How are your plans coming along?" He asked.

"Pretty well, I'm just waiting to hear back from Marco whether he will meet me and provide a place and time, under an alias, of course."

"Of course," he repeated.

More awkward silence.

"I wish I was going with you," Chad finally said.

"Me, too. Maybe next time," I replied.

He looked at me and smiled. "Sure, when you move in with your Italian side of the family, don't forget about us, little people."

I nudged him with my shoulder, "Never."

We talked a little more about other stuff, mundane things. He was going to change his car's oil this weekend, I needed to confirm my rental in Rome, he was playing soccer with some buddies next week while I was gone. It was all an effort to avoid talking about the fact that we were both scared.

The unknown was always frightening if you dwelled on it too much. We were both desperately trying to occupy our thoughts with other, unimportant things. He was in a rut and I felt like my legs were dangling on the edge of the dock. Perhaps if we didn't voice these things out loud, they wouldn't be real. But they were very real.

"Well, I'd better get back," I said as I stood up. He gave me a hug and we waved good night as I went inside my house with Bear.

THE EMAIL FROM MARCO didn't come until two days later. My heart was racing when I saw his name in my inbox. I was too nervous to open it and actually paced the room a few times before I did. I took a deep breath and clicked on the message.

"Dear Ms. Gabriella Delaney,

I must first say my apology. My English is not very good.

We are happy to get your email. Wine is our passion. Cosimo is not in good health but I am happy to see you when you come to Frascati. Mornings are good. Come ten o'clock at this address.

Ciao,

Marco Vernetti"

Under the body of the email was an address. I couldn't believe it had worked! I had an invitation with a day and time. I was very concerned when he said Cosimo wasn't in good health. It was probably a good thing I was coming sooner rather than later. If I never had the chance to meet him or even talk with him I would be devastated.

I just sat back in my chair and looked at my computer screen. My half-brother just sent me an email and I don't even think he knows it. He may figure it out, since I'm not actually sending any wine, but by then it won't matter. I want them to know who I am.

My next email was to confirm my rental with Antonio Rossi. If nothing else, I needed to make sure I had a place to stay. It was short and sweet, just confirming dates and times. Now I was getting excited. I still had nerves and butterflies in my stomach, but I was also really looking forward to this trip.

I texted my friends to see how their plans were coming along. They were excited to be heading to Mexico, but also sad that I wasn't coming along. I wished I was going with them, too. We haven't hung out all together since the fourth of July. I missed them but promised to meet up after our respective trips to exchange stories.

I filled them in on my email from Marco and they were so excited for me. We were all a little surprised that the bogus email actually worked. It was my way to meet him, but it didn't guarantee that I would be able to talk to Cosimo or get any information. Especially if he was ill.

Jenny confirmed that the new guy in the pictures was her new boyfriend, Mike. We all wished her well and hoped it worked out. Jenny said she might be getting a promotion soon that would allow her to travel with various news stories, so that was exciting to hear. I told her that I would know she made it when I saw her on the television.

We continued to text until they started sending me Italian phrases that I would never say to any guy while I was there! I laughed and said good bye to them all. I was not going there to get a boyfriend, this trip was much more personal.

I went downstairs to grab something to eat. I made a sandwich and went into the living room to watch tv. Mom was in her corner chair crocheting a blanket.

"Hi honey," she said.

"Hi, mom, do you mind if I turn on the tv?"

"No, go right ahead."

I kept glancing over at her while scrolling through the channels. She never acted suspicious of my trip and I wondered what she would say if she knew I was going to Italy instead of Mexico. There were a million times over the last few months that I wanted to tell her, but didn't. It wasn't the time. She would catch me looking at her a few times.

"So, is everything ready for your trip to Cancun?" She asked.

"I think so. I'm leaving in a few days, so ready or not, I'm going."

Her hands kept moving with the yarn and crochet hook. There were no underlying tones to her speech, no hint at all that she suspected. I was glad for that. I hated lying to her and everyone in my family, but I needed answers that she couldn't or wouldn't give me. I needed to hear from Cosimo.

I had found a sappy romance movie and was only half paying attention. I kept looking at my email from Marco, when I saw a new email in my inbox. It was from Antonio and he was confirming my apartment rental. I was so excited that I must have said something out loud.

"Good news?" Mom asked.

Taken by surprise, I couldn't tell her what it was really about. "Oh, yes, Jenny has a boyfriend. His name is Mike."

"Oh, isn't that nice," Mom replied.

"Yes, it is," I answered.

Afraid that I might still let something slip out, I decided it was best to go back to my room. "Good night, mom," I said as I walked over and gave her a hug and kiss on the cheek.

"Good night, Luna."

I wasn't really tired, but my room was probably the safest place for me the next couple of days. I had come too far to make any mistakes now. My luggage was packed and sitting in the corner. I had my sunhat and Mexico travel guide sitting on top. I would leave those in Chad's car when he took me to the airport.

That reminded me, I'd better confirm the date and time with Chad. With everything going on in his head, he could still forget about me. I decided to call him rather than text.

"Hey, Luna."

"Hi," I replied. "I'm just checking to make sure things are still on for us this Sunday."

I heard his deep laugh. "Yes, Luna. It's only been in my calendar for two months. I won't forget. I will get you safely to the airport and pick you up the following week. You are still planning to come back, right?"

"Very funny," I replied. Then added, "Maybe."

It was good to hear Chad laugh. I didn't hear it often enough. We said goodnight and hung up.

Chapter 12

Today was the day! All of my planning and preparations were leading up to today. I was a bundle of nerves all morning. I couldn't even eat breakfast but packed a sandwich for later. My flight was at three and Chad was taking me at one. I cleaned up my bedroom and took Bear out for a walk.

Everyone promised that they would take care of Bear while I was away. Even Alice said she would take him out when she got home from work each night. Alice was enjoying her summer job at the amusement park, but it was long hours. I thought we would be able to spend more time together this summer, but it didn't work out that way.

It was a warm day. Normally I would be out in shorts and a t-shirt, but I couldn't wear that on the plane. Instead, I opted for nice loose-fitting black pants and a short sleeved navy blue shirt. I knew airplanes could be chilly, so it wouldn't looks strange for someone who was supposed to be going to Mexico to be wearing pants.

At one o'clock I walked over to Chad's car. He was coming out of his house dangling his keys in front of my face.

"Your chariot awaits," he joked.

He helped put my luggage in the trunk and I got in. I was ready. No longer anxious, nervous or scared, I was definitely ready. Chad started the car and we headed towards the airport.

"Good luck," he said. "I hope you find the answers you're looking for, you deserve it."

"Thank you. I hope so, too."

"If you need anything, just text me," he said.

"Just remember, if my family asks any questions, I'm in Cancun this week." I replied.

"No problem, you can count on me."

I could and I knew it. I could trust Chad with my life. Sometimes I feel like I have. He dropped me off, we hugged and then he was off. Erie International Airport wasn't very big. It was only a matter of minutes before I was checked in, passed security and was sitting at my gate. I had brought a book with me and started reading.

There was something about sitting at the gate in an airport that made me feel grown up. Maybe it was the fact that I was doing this all alone, but I felt like one of these business travelers who were off on important business. I was twenty-two and going out into the world for the first time by myself. I told myself to enjoy the adventure.

When they called us for boarding, I felt calm. The gate agent scanned my ticket and gestured toward the airplane. I sat in my window seat and settled in for the short flight before connecting to my longer flight to Rome. There wasn't any food service, so I was glad I packed my sandwich.

My flight to Rome had some turbulence but it didn't last long. There was a nice older couple in my row. The woman next to me was chatty at first, which concerned me. I didn't want to be seated next to one of those travelers who wanted to talk the whole flight. Thankfully, she wasn't. Once we had our first drink service, I was relieved when she settled down and watched a movie.

I watched several. Unable to sleep, I ate when they brought us food and had some wine. I was learning that international flights were pretty nice. As we got closer to our destination, I did doze off. More of a nap than an actual night's sleep, but it would have to do. It was already mid-morning in Rome and I had the whole day ahead of me.

Once we landed, it took a few minutes to get my bearings. I passed through customs and immigration without any problem and then I was confronted with my transportation choices into the city. I knew I needed to take the express train so once on board, I relaxed for the next hour until I reached the center of Rome.

As I stepped off the train at Roma Termini station, I was immediately hit with the sights and smells of Italy. I could smell espresso coming from the nearby coffee shop, the aroma of fresh pizza coming across the street and the horns of the cars driving by on the busy roads. I couldn't help but smile and take it all in.

I quickly learned that I needed to keep moving when people were bumping into me as I was standing on the sidewalk. I was looking up the way to my apartment rental and then I headed in that direction. Turn right, walk one block, then turn left and it is on your left. The apartment building was number twenty-five and next to it was a pizzeria.

I knew I was a little early, according to the check in time Antonio provided in his email, so I decided to eat first. I was starving and it smelled delicious. I pulled my suitcase to the front door and asked for a table. The hostess asked if I wanted to sit inside or outside.

"Outside, please," I replied.

She led me to a small round table with two chairs. I placed my carry on bag on the seat and squeezed my luggage between the two chairs. When I sat down to look at the menu, I simply couldn't focus. There were people walking by that I imagined were going for high fashion photo shoots or on their way to Gucci or Prada to do some shopping.

My waiter came up to me with a pen and notepad. I hadn't even given the menu a cursory glance but my instinct told me to order pizza. My waiter didn't have a name tag on, but he was tall and very handsome. Rome was turning out to be my favorite city in the world.

"English?" He asked.

"Yes, I'm American."

He took one look at my suitcase and asked if I was leaving or arriving. I told him I was staying at the apartment next door. He gave a nod of recognition. He must meet lots of tourists from that apartment.

"Ah, yes, of course. Do you want to start off with a drink?" He asked.

"Sure," I said, still not knowing what the menu offered. "I'll have a white wine."

He smiled. "Perfect! Do you know what you would like to order?"

"Yes, pizza."

This time he laughed. His smile was beautiful. His head tipped back a bit when he laughed and his short, dark curly hair bounced in the breeze. His brown eyes squinted in amusement as his whole face became softer.

"I'm sorry," I replied. "That was stupid of me. I'll have a small cheese pizza, please."

"Very good," he said. "I'll be right back with your wine." He took the menu and returned into the restaurant.

Goodness, five minutes in Italy and I'm already a stereotype. I was just so excited to be here, on a street cafe ordering my own lunch. I took some pictures and a couple selfies to send back to my friends. Careful not to include my family. I would forward pictures that Trish, Nancy and Jenny sent to me, to my parents.

My waiter brought me my white wine and I sipped it until my pizza arrived. It was probably the most beautiful pizza I had ever seen. It tasted amazing, too. I noticed that other tables around me were eating pasta, fish and soup so I knew if I wanted to eat here again, it wouldn't have to be just pizza. Maybe I would actually read the menu next time.

I savored every sip and every bite. Sitting at this outdoor restaurant made me realize that I could get used to this. I looked at the time and asked for the check. I paid, took my luggage and walked into the apartment building next door. I punched in the code that Antonio had sent me and retrieved my key.

The apartment was on the second floor with no elevator, at least it wasn't the fifth floor. Inside the apartment I found it to be cute, a little small but perfect. There were windows that opened and faced the street and it even had a small balcony. I put my luggage in the bedroom, hung up some clothes and kicked off my shoes. I laid on the bed and relaxed. All of the work and effort it took to get here was finally worth it.

I saw that Antonio had a note posted by the door that listed his phone number in case I needed anything. As I looked around, I was sure I didn't know how many of these appliances worked so I may have to give him a call later. I didn't want to just sit inside the rest of the day so I changed clothes and went out to explore.

With no destination in mind, I just roamed around and popped inside little shops along the way. I had pistachio gelato, bought myself a journal and found a tourist information booth that provide me with a map. Now, I just needed to choose a direction.

I continued walking away from my apartment and tried to stay out of people's way. It was August, so there were a lot of tourists from all over the world. I could hear bits of French, Spanish and even Japanese as I made my way through the streets.

As I stood at an intersection waiting for the light to change I took a moment to look around. I had been looking down at my map most of the way trying to figure out where I was. That's when I spotted the large, round and very familiar shape of the Colosseum. No wonder so many people were waiting at this crosswalk.

I followed the sea of people down the hill and stood in front of this ancient marvel. Behind me was the Roman Forum. Places I have only seen in history books or on the internet. It was late in the day and the line was long, so instead of trying to get in, I walked around it. I took pictures and selfies before wanting to sit down.

This was amazing. My first day here and I've already seen more than I could ever imagine. I found a street vendor selling some pastries so I bought two with a bottle of water. As I sat and admired my view of the Colosseum, I sent a picture to Chad.

It was getting late and I wanted to return before it got too dark. I walked back the way I came and stopped at a small grocery store to pick up some snacks and food for tomorrow. Back at the apartment, I put my food away and took a shower. I dug out the new journal I purchased today and wrote my first entry.

I described everything about the flight, the pizza and my walk. I had a lot to write. I wanted to remember this trip for as long as I lived. Especially if things didn't go my way, this may be the last time I came here. My plan was to enjoy every moment of every day.

I noticed that Chad had texted me back, 'Wow'. That was the perfect word to sum up my day. I was tired and I hoped that jet lag wouldn't give me any problems sleeping tonight.

I turned off the lights and crawled into bed. I laid there listening to the sounds of the cars, scooters and people on the street continuing on into the night. It lulled me into a peaceful and deep sleep. Goodnight, Rome, I will see you tomorrow.

Chapter 13

I woke up to the sun shining through my window. I slept great and was eager to get out of bed. I had put a little more effort into planning my itinerary for today. I used the food I had intended for my breakfast and packed it for my lunch instead. I wanted to eat breakfast at the restaurant downstairs.

I put on a sundress and sandals and went down to eat. The same waiter was there to show me to my table. He smiled at me and gave me the menu. This time I took the time to read it properly. When he came over to take my order, I was ready.

"Buongiorno," he said with a smile. "What can I get you this morning?"

"Good morning," I replied. "I would like a cappuccino, a chocolate croissant and dish of fresh fruit, please."

"Yes, of course," he said and returned into the restaurant.

When he came out with my cappuccino, he saw that I was reading my tourist map. "Where are you planning to go today?" He asked.

"Well, I think I'm going to go back to the Colosseum. I went yesterday, but didn't get to go inside. Then I will explore the Forum. After that I will just have to see..." I let my sentence trail off because I really didn't know much beyond that.

"Perfect!" He replied. "You will enjoy it."

"Thank you."

He brought out the rest of my order and I watched as people walked by, starting their day. I was one of them now. I would be walking the streets of Rome with a destination and a purpose. I had tucked my journal into my backpack and took it out to start writing about my morning. After paying, I grabbed my backpack and headed down the street.

I purchased tickets for both the Colosseum and the Forum and stood in line. It was still early, so the line was short. Inside was incredible. There were many levels inside the Colosseum and the steps where huge. It was so hard to believe that I was walking inside of a building that was centuries old. I let my hands run along the old stone walls.

When I got to the inside rim of the stadium, I was speechless. The floor showed hidden rooms where animals or gladiators were kept. The walls were crumbling after centuries and yet, you got a feel for the way it must have felt back then. History came to life with the pictures and descriptions along the outside walls.

I took lots of pictures and then just stood back and took it all in. After a few hours, I exited the Colosseum and sat on the grass. I pulled my lunch from my backpack and ate under the shade of a large tree.

It was easy to get caught up in the romance of it all. However, as soon as I started thinking of the real reason I was here, I started to feel a knot in my stomach. I purposely planned my meeting with Marco to be towards the end of my trip so regardless of whether it went well or not, I would still enjoy myself first.

I toured the Roman Forum and found my guide book to be extremely helpful when it came to descriptions and anecdotes. I would never have known what I was looking at or its significance to history without the words on the page. I was walking in the footsteps of Caesar himself.

I had spent another couple of hours there before heading back up the street. I spotted a large white building that was a monument to Italy's first king. It looked a bit like a large wedding cake. I had to check it out.

I crossed the street and went up the stairs that led to a very large, flat landing. It provided an amazing view of the ancient city. I took some more pictures and returned back towards my apartment.

I stopped into the small grocery store again and purchased more food for tonight and tomorrow. I promised myself that I would plan even better for tomorrow. Maybe even venture onto a train or a bus.

In the apartment, I laid down on the bed, suddenly very tired. Maybe my jet lag was catching up with me after all. I curled up and fell asleep. When I awoke, I noticed the sun was much lower in the sky. It was dinner time already.

I had purchased a can of soup at the store that looked delicious. I had gotten some bread to eat with it, I just needed to heat it up. I found a small saucepan and emptied the soup into it. It was when I was trying to turn on the stove that I knew I needed help. I considered turning random knobs, but I didn't want to burn down Antonio's house.

I picked up the phone and dialed the number on the wall.

"Buona sera," Antonio said.

"Hello?" I replied.

"Hello, good evening," Antonio corrected himself. "Can I help you?"

"Yes, my name is Luna and I'm staying in your apartment rental number twenty-five."

"Of course," he said. "How is everything?"

I explained that I loved the apartment and the city but I am having trouble with the stove. I didn't know how to say that in Italian, so he said he would be right over to help in person. I didn't have to wait long until there was a knock on the door.

When I opened the door, I couldn't believe my eyes. My gasp must have startled him, but his sly smile let me know that he wasn't surprised.

"You're the waiter from downstairs!" I said, still trying to figure out why he was here.

"Yes, I am Antonio Rossi, how can I help you, Luna?" He asked with a smile that was as dashing up close as it was from a distance.

"Did you know who I was this whole time?" I wondered. Of course he did, the reservation required a copy of my passport. He had my picture the entire time.

"Well, yes." He answered. "I'm sorry I did not introduce myself yesterday, I was very busy."

I found myself staring at his eyes. Antonio was handsome and not much older than me, I guessed. It was convenient that he worked next door. He was still standing in the entry way and started looking around. I suddenly remembered that I had called him about the stove.

"Right, anyway," I stammered. "I tried to heat up soup and I don't know how." I felt like an idiot. Was English my second language, too? "I mean, how does the stove work?"

"Yes, of course, no problem," he said. Antonio showed me how to use the stove and then hesitated before leaving. "What are your plans tomorrow?"

I gestured to my guidebook on the table and my map. "I'm starting to plan that out now."

"No, no, no," he said. "I will take you."

I didn't know what he meant, exactly. I didn't know where I was going, so I didn't know where he would take me. I protested but he insisted.

"I show you Rome!" He announced. He placed a hand on his chest like it was a vow. "Please, I don't want you to go alone in Rome."

I was ready to protest one last time before I imagined what my friends would say in this instance. They would say, 'Go for it'. Why not? He didn't look dangerous. "Okay," I finally answered.

Antonio's face lit up. "Perfect!" He said. "I meet you downstairs at eight and I show you Rome!" He stood there watching me and I was staring right back. He was taller than me and his curly dark hair was falling down over his forehead. He took a step closer to me and put out his hand. I took it.

"Until tomorrow," he said and kissed the back of my hand.

Even after he turned and left the apartment, I still felt him there. His face, his cologne and his touch lingered in my head all evening. Antonio probably acted like this with all of his renters.

I ate my dinner and immediately texted my friends. They were typing in all caps when I said I met a sexy Italian man. It was fun to think about, but he was probably married or something like that. I would just enjoy the day out with a local man and then focus on my meeting with Marco and Cosimo later that week.

I was feeling restless and I wasn't ready to go to bed, yet. I went back outside and took a walk. I imagined I was walking Bear. What would he make of all these sights and sounds? I found another gelato shop and got mango gelato in a cone.

I walked in a different direction than this morning and found a park. It was dark now, but I didn't feel unsafe. There were so many people walking around, street vendors on every corner and plenty of restaurants still serving customers. The city still had a life after dark.

I had a text message on my phone and saw it was Chad. 'Are you up?'

I decided to make it easier and video called him. He answered right away. I showed him that I was sitting in a park eating a gelato at night. He was both impressed and jealous. I missed him and I think he missed me, too. I asked if everything was okay and he said it was, he was just wondering how things were going.

"Well, the guy who owns the apartment is going to show me around all day tomorrow."

"Wait, what?" His voice turned suddenly harsh.

I laughed, he could be just like a big brother sometimes. "He's harmless I think, besides, I can handle myself."

Chad laughed and confirmed that I could. He said my parents asked if he had heard from me at all. He told them that I was having a great time on the beach. I laughed and thanked him. He was saving my butt, again. I tried to ask him, again, how he was doing, but he changed the subject.

I stayed video talking to him as I walked back to my apartment. He commented on the people and the restaurants as I walked down the streets. I asked him what he wanted me to bring him back from Italy and he just said that he wanted me to come back safely. He didn't need anything. Well, I was still going to get him something anyway.

I showed him my apartment for the week, complete with a full tour of every room. He loved it, then he said he had to get back to work. We hung up and I went to take my shower. I wrote in my journal all about my day. I even mentioned my plans for tomorrow. I stopped to consider what I was going to wear.

Without knowing where we were going and how much walking we would do, I considered many different options. I had brought a few dresses and a couple pairs of pants, but also several pairs of shorts. I decided to wear my white shorts and red top. I laid them out and imagined spending the day with Antonio. With him as my tour guide, I didn't really care where we went.

I laid in bed and flipped through the channels on tv. There were quite a few stations that had programs in English but I wasn't sure what I was in the mood for. I decided to watch an old movie that I had seen a dozen times. There was just something comforting about it.

I went back into the kitchen to grab a snack and a drink. I brought it all back to the bed and enjoyed my evening with the tv. I really didn't think I was very tired, especially since I had an unexpected nap in the middle of the afternoon, but I did not get to finish the end of the movie.

Chapter 14

Today I woke up with such enthusiasm that anyone would have automatically assumed that I was going on a date. Well, maybe I was. I just knew I would get to see more of Rome today. I ate breakfast in the apartment this morning and threw a snack and a drink in my backpack. At eight o'clock, I ran downstairs.

There was a man sitting on a cute white Vespa right outside the door. I looked up and down the street, right past him, until the man took off his helmet.

"Antonio! What is this?" I asked, surprised.

"Buongiorno, Luna! This is your ride today."

I stood looking at the Italian scooter and wondered if he was serious. He was. Antonio produced another helmet and held it out to me. I hesitated so he got off the scooter.

"You don't like?" He asked.

"I don't know, I've never been on one," I replied, cautiously taking the helmet from him.

"Perfect! We go for the first time," Antonio answered, so happy that I was willing to ride with him.

I sat on the seat with Antonio. He took my hands and brought them in front of him. "Hold on," he instructed. I simply nodded my head and locked my hands together in front of him.

As we pulled away from the curb and out into the traffic, I closed my eyes. He tried to talk to me as we rode down the cobblestone streets, but with the wind, the noise and my heart beating so loudly in my ears, I couldn't hear a word he said.

Antonio weaved between cars and beeped his horn when they cut him off. It was frightening and thrilling all at the same time. I felt like I was in a movie with a stunt driver. He drove up a small alleyway and then came to a stop. He was removing his helmet and held out his hand for mine.

"Where are we?" I asked.

"Look," he said, gesturing to a large stone water fountain. "This is Trevi Fountain."

It was beautiful. We walked closer as the sound of the water got louder. Crowds of people blocked the view, but Antonio cleared a path. He elbowed his way to the front and handed me a coin. I was too distracted by the marble figures in front of me.

He explained that the tradition was to turn your back to the fountain and throw the coin over your shoulder. It means you will return to Rome and have good luck in life and love. I wasn't sure one coin could ensure all of that, but it was worth a try. I heard the splash and Antonio gave me a hug.

I took lots of pictures and even got Antonio in a few. We got back on the scooter and rode through town, again. I was starting to feel more secure on the back of his bike. He obviously had lots of practice and he knew the streets. I really didn't have anything to worry about.

My death grip loosened. I let my hands relax and rest on Antonio's chest and stomach. I felt his muscles under his shirt and smelled his cologne. It was intoxicating to be here with him. We had arrived at our next destination and walked around the corner. Even with crowds I recognized this place.

The Spanish Steps led up to a church. There were too many people sitting on the steps to easily ascend, so we took pictures at the bottom. There was more to see, but it was lunch time and we were hungry. He said he knew a place near here that had the best pasta in Rome.

We only walked half a block before we entered this little restaurant with amazing smells. "Tony!" A man in a white chef's uniform called from the back.

"Luigi!" Antonio called back. I followed him to a table in the back and he ordered, "The usual."

"Tony?" I asked. He said all of his friends called him Tony and that I could, too. This made me blush and I wasn't sure why. He got up to order a bottle of wine and came back with two glasses.

"This is the white wine you like," Tony said. "It is from near here," he gestured with his arms outstretched.

It was delicious and fruity, the same wine I had at the restaurant he worked at the first night. We sipped our wine and I caught him staring at me several times. This made me blush even more.

"Tell me about yourself," I said to him.

Tony set his glass down and leaned back. He said he was twenty-eight and single. He works everyday and enjoys it. If he needs extra money, he rents his apartment out and stays with his family.

"So do you give private tours to all of your customers?" I asked with a smile.

"No!" Tony said, "You are the first one." He looked almost like I insulted him. I believed him.

Luigi brought our pasta dinners to the table. The aroma made my stomach growl. Luigi grated some cheese on top and we dug in. Tony was eating slowly and enjoying every bite. I twirled mine on the fork and took big mouthfuls. The whole outside world disappeared. At this moment, there was only the wine, the pasta and Antonio.

Luigi wouldn't take any money. He hugged Tony and we left. We wound our way through more small streets and alleyways. I kept my hands on Antonio's abs the whole time. We stopped at the Pantheon and went inside. I was in awe as we gazed up from the center of the dome. I wondered at the engineering feats that created such beautiful structures in Italy.

"Gelato time," Tony said.

This time I got two flavors, coffee and raspberry. Tony got blueberry and lemon. I let him taste mine and I tasted his. I don't think our eyes left each other's face the whole time. There was definitely an attraction between us, but I did not need a boyfriend in Italy.

As we sat on a bench watching the Pantheon, he asked me what my plans for tomorrow were. I explained briefly that I needed to be in Frascati tomorrow at ten. I was going to find out which train I needed to take. He asked why I needed to go to Frascati, it was not a typical tourist destination.

"I'm meeting Cosimo Vernetti," I replied. I was looking down at my phone, sure he couldn't guess my real reason for going. I tried to sound casual, sure that Antonio didn't know who he was.

What I didn't see was Antonio's eyes widen at the name. "Do you know him?" He asked.

"No," I replied as casually as possible. "I am meeting him for the first time." Then I noticed a different look on Tony's face. "Do you know him?"

"No, not personally." Tony studied my face for a moment and then said, "I will take you."

I tried to protest but he insisted. It would be such a long and unfamiliar journey, he wanted to make sure I got there without any problems. I reluctantly gave in only after making him promise that I paid for his gas and all meals tomorrow. He agreed to those terms and smiled.

His smile was contagious. The sun was getting lower and he said we should head back. I hated for this day to end, but I knew I would see him again tomorrow. I actually felt excited at the idea of spending another whole day with Antonio.

We didn't drive straight back to the apartment, he took a long scenic route. At one point, he stopped on the side of the road that looked down onto the city lights. It was breathtaking. There was one time when our faces were so close together that I thought he might try to kiss me, but he didn't. I wouldn't have minded.

It was late when we arrived back in front of the apartment. The restaurant next door was closed.

"Are you hungry?" He asked.

"Yes," I replied.

"Follow me." Antonio pulled out his key ring and opened the front door to the restaurant. We made our way to the kitchen and he turned on the lights.

"Are you allowed to be in here?" I asked, concerned that the police would show up.

"Yes," he said with a smirk. "This is my restaurant."

I let that statement sink in while Antonio floated around the kitchen. He was in his element. It was my stupid assumption that he only worked here. That was why he said he worked everyday. He was the owner. He was the chef.

Antonio pulled food out of the fridge, and threw things into hot pans on the stove. He added sauces and spices and worked his magic. When he was finished, he brought out two dishes and placed them on the stainless steel table between us.

It was a shrimp and pasta dish that he just whipped up in twenty minutes. The smell of the butter and garlic made my mouth water. He brought a few rolls and some butter to add to the table arrangement. "Perfect!" He said.

This whole day was perfect. I don't think I could ever top such a perfect day in my life. I took a picture of the food before we started eating. No one was going to believe me unless I showed them the proof.

The single overhead lamp provided the perfect ambiance to our intimate dinner. I was falling for Antonio and but I didn't want to.

He was not in the plan. How was I going to say good bye to him in a few days? I had to protect my heart.

I didn't know what Antonio's intentions were, but I could certainly guess his feelings. He kept watching me as I watched him. I tried to help clean up the dishes but he insisted that I leave them. His father came in early in the morning and checked on things. His father was the one who started the restaurant, but Antonio took it over last year.

He stayed with his dad on the first floor of the apartment building when he rented his out during the busy seasons. It was convenient and smart.

"Where's your mother?" I asked.

Antonio hesitated. "She passed away a couple of years ago. That is why my father gave up the restaurant. His heart just wasn't in it any longer."

"I'm sorry," I replied.

He said they were doing better and moving forward. "Life goes on."

Our conversation was so intimate and personal. I felt like I was really getting to know Tony. I may never see this man again in my life, so I took a chance, too.

"I wasn't completely honest with you earlier," I said.

His confused look was genuine. "What do you mean?"

"The reason I'm going to Frascati is to see my father, Cosimo Dante Vernetti." I looked up at Tony and he put his hand to his opened mouth.

"Seriously?" He asked. "Do you know who he is?" When I shook my head, no, Tony stood up and brought over the open bottle of white wine we had been drinking. The same wine I've been drinking the last few days in Italy. "Look at the label."

Vernetti Vineyards. I looked closer at the image on the label. It wasn't just a circle surrounding the words, it was a moon, a full moon. I looked up at Antonio and back again at the label. Did Cosimo know? Was this a coincidence that there was a moon on the label? I felt like I already knew the answers, but I wouldn't admit them to myself until I spoke with him directly.

"Luna means moon, no?" Antonio made the connection long before I did. Probably even at the moment I said Cosimo's name.

I didn't even know I was crying until Tony handed me a napkin. "Yes, it does," I replied. "I wasn't sure he even knew I existed. Do you think this was on purpose?"

"No one knows for sure why Vernetti Vineyards has a moon on the label. It has always been there as long as I can remember," said Tony.

It has probably been there twenty-two years. The knot was returning and it was getting bigger. What was I getting myself into? Could it be a secret code? I was the Russian defector, again. One ping only.

Chapter 15

Antonio would be picking me up at nine o'clock. I was pleasantly surprised when he was parked outside in a car, not the scooter. I had chosen to wear a dress because I wanted to make a good impression. On who, though, Antonio or Cosimo? It was overcast today but it wasn't supposed to rain.

The ride would take us about an hour. Antonio gestured to a bag next to him that was full of croissants and also an iced coffee.

"Thank you!" I said.

"We must start this journey to meet your father off properly," Tony said.

I savored the buttery croissants and enjoyed the scenery. We were heading out of the city and everything was turning more green and lush. Eventually, grass and trees turned to grapes with acres of vineyards on both sides of the road.

Antonio's sports car handled the winding roads with ease. The ride was smooth but I was a bundle of nerves inside. He must have sensed it because he took my hand. It was nothing more than moral support, or was it? I wasn't sure how I felt about holding hands, so when he swerved to avoid a pot hole, he put both hands back on the steering wheel.

It was probably for the best. I already decided that no matter what he said, I would spend my last day in Italy alone. Two full days with Antonio was enough. I didn't want to get attached. I had enough to deal with when I got home, like some hard questions for my mother. I wondered how she could have taken me away from my father.

I had always given her the benefit of the doubt, that maybe she didn't know she was pregnant and had already returned to the States and didn't tell him. Or, maybe he knew but didn't want me. All of the scenarios I had come up with in the past didn't fit anymore. There was a moon, he knew and he was broadcasting it to the world.

We were getting closer, I could tell. Antonio pulled over at a café and asked if I was okay. I was sad, mad and scared. "Yes, I'm okay," I replied. That was easier to understand than what was really going on inside of me right now.

I got out and walked around the car. I was starting to hyperventilate and Tony came over and gave me a hug. He sensed I was falling apart. He held me tight as if he could hold me together. It felt good, but it wasn't enough. Some things would always remain broken. The damage had started twenty-two years ago.

We both eventually returned to the car and he kept driving. He checked his location and confirmed that this was the address Marco provided. It was an imposing house, very grand from the outside and I was sure the inside matched it. We stayed in the car. There was still fifteen minutes until our meeting time with Marco and Cosimo.

There was still time to turn around and go home. I didn't have to do this. I could potentially be putting myself in a position of being rejected, again. But I didn't think that was the case. I think he knows and was reaching out. This internal conflict was becoming too much.

"Let's do this," I said as I got out of the car. I was more than ready to finally find out the truth from my father.

Tony grabbed both of my arms, "Are you sure?"

"Yes," I replied with a confidence I wasn't sure was real.

Tony walked up the front stairs with me but rather than join me inside, he would stay outside. He was giving me the space and privacy I needed. I knocked on the very large wooden double doors. An older gentleman answered the door.

"Hello, I'm Gabriella Delaney to see Marco and Cosimo Vernetti."

"Come in," the man said as he stepped aside and gestured for me to enter the foyer. It was opulent with gold everywhere. If this was the foyer, I could only imagine what the rest of the house looked like. I was walking around the perimeter of the room when I heard footsteps coming down the hall.

I turned to see a young man, tall and handsome. He couldn't be more than eighteen or nineteen and he had the same dark hair and eyes as me.

"Hello, I'm Marco Vernetti," he said, extending his right hand.

I shook it. "Hello, I'm Gabriella Delaney."

Marco had a calm demeanor and gestured for me to walk with him back down the hall.

"I'm sorry to say your wine never arrived," Marco said.

It took me a minute to remember that in the email I had asked for the address in order to send wine for them to taste. I suddenly felt extremely guilty for the lies. Marco didn't suspect anything, then. I wasn't sure if he would know me or the name, but he really didn't seem to have any recognition of either.

Marco led me into a larger room with more gold framed portraits and velvet curtains. On one side of the room was a long table with several bottles of wine and glasses. We walked over and stood in front of the display. Marco had arranged his own wine tasting for me.

"I would like you to try this wine," Marco said. He nodded for a man in uniform to come over and pour for them. Marco handed me one and he took the other.

I sipped the wine and it was very familiar. It was the same wine I had been drinking with Antonio. "It's delicious," I said.

"Good, good," Marco replied. He gestured for another bottle to be poured, "Now this one." He watched me as I sipped each glass.

We continued tasting wonderful wine for nearly an hour. It was very nice, but the whole time I was observing Marco. We had similar looks and mannerisms, but our upbringing couldn't have been more opposite. If he found out we were siblings, would he assume I was raised like this? I was the daughter of Cosimo Vernetti, why wouldn't all of his children have servants?

We didn't. Some of us didn't even know we were his child until a couple of months ago. I was wondering when Cosimo would join us. Where was he? I was glad to meet Marco, but I didn't come all this way to sip wine with my half-brother.

"May I ask if Cosimo will be joining us?" I asked finally.

Marco put his glass down and explained, again, that he was in bad health. He needed to look up a word in order to say it in English. Stroke. I had to set my glass down, too. It was worse than I thought.

Marco explained that his left side is not working and that he must use a breathing tube and has monitors by his bed. He was currently asleep but one of his servants would inform him when he woke up. That was what they were waiting for.

It was good and bad news. Cosimo was here, but wouldn't be able to talk. I would not get any answers, not unless they could take his breathing tube out in the next few minutes. It was devastating. I came all this way for nothing and I felt foolish and stupid. I should be on a beach in Mexico right now.

Marco must have sensed a change in my body language because he grew concerned. "It is okay. The doctors think he will get better. There are small signs each day."

"Okay," I answered.

Marco wasn't convinced that it was. "He should be awake soon. You will see yourself."

Just then another man in a black suit entered the room. "He is ready, sir."

Marco smiled, "Let us go see my father. I must warn you that he probably will still be sleepy and won't be able to talk. I told him you were coming, of course, but there wasn't much reaction."

My father. This was it. The knots were returning and getting bigger. I prayed me feet could make the journey across the hallway without bolting down the hall and out the door. The man opened another set of lavish wooden doors and I followed Marco inside.

The room was more stuffy and dark than the other room we had just left. I could hear the soft beeping of machines and the rhythmic movement of the ventilator. When Marco said they were waiting for him to wake up, I didn't realize he slept in one of the downstairs rooms. But now that I saw the silhouette of a hospital bed with matching equipment, I understood why.

Marco asked the man to open a few curtains. As light filtered into the dimly lit room I could see a man lying on the hospital bed. It was slightly elevated and it was facing the windows. I slowly and quietly approached him from his right side.

I knew I was in Cosimo's line of vision when his eyes widened. His eyes followed mine as I came around in front of him. I looked for any sign of recognition. I searched his face and I could see hints of my nose and chin. He was covered in blankets and tubes, so I couldn't get a good sense of his height or physical build.

Marco was busying himself with the servants and other instructions. I stayed near my father. I came up very close to him and whispered, "Hello, it's me, Luna Gabriella. I've come to see you and meet you. I'm very sorry you are ill and I hope you get better."

I searched his face and could not detect any change. Did he understand what I just said to him? Maybe he didn't speak any English. I never thought to ask Marco that. Marco spoke English, why wouldn't Cosimo?

I left Cosimo's side and walked towards the windows. So, this was his view each day? It was so lush and green. What a beautiful place to live and grow up! I returned to my father's side. Marco was still busy with other business.

"Do you remember Shirley? She is my mother," I whispered to Cosimo.

There was one beep that was getting faster, perhaps that was his heart rate monitor. I didn't want to get him angry. I just wanted answers and it was getting more and more frustrating to be right here next to the man who could provide them but couldn't. If I did anything to affect Cosimo's health, Marco would have me thrown out.

I turned back towards my father. There was a slight movement that I saw in the corner of my eye. I went back to his right side, his strong side. He was moving his fingers and slowly raising his arm. His eyes never left my face.

Marco had left the room, some other emergency must have needed his attention. I looked back down at my father's hand that he was slowly bringing up. I didn't know what he was trying to do. Was there an emergency call button he wanted to press? Was he kicking me out?

I hesitated before I reached for his hand. I wasn't sure if that was what he wanted, but I took the chance. One ping only. I put my hand in his and he squeezed. It wasn't a hard squeeze but I felt it. Was he just doing this as a handshake?

I wondered if I should go and get Marco, but I didn't. Something in the way he held my hand told me this was a friendly gesture. I held my father's hand and squeezed back. I still didn't know if he knew who I was or what I was doing here, but I stayed by his side and held his hand.

I was about to give up and let go until I saw it. Sliding down his right cheek, his good side, was one single tear. I was shocked. That tear was followed by another one until he was crying. So was I. He knew. He knew who I was.

I bent down and gave him a kiss on the forehead. "Hello, father," I said. He squeezed my hand again and I squeezed back. One ping only.

Chapter 16

The last thing I remember was bursting out of the room and running down the long hallway. When I exited the grand foyer, I searched for Antonio. He knew who I was! I kept saying it in my head. He remembered me!

I quickly scanned the larger veranda and spotted Antonio in the far corner. He was leaning on the concrete railing and was looking out over the vineyard. I ran to him. He must have heard my approach because as soon as he turned to me I jumped in his arms. "He knew me!"

I didn't realize that Marco was running behind me the whole time. When Tony released me, I turned to see Marco with concern on his face. My own face was a whirlwind of emotions. I was both laughing and crying at the same time.

Marco hesitated before speaking, "Is everything okay? Did something happen?"

I turned back towards Antonio, "It was perfect!"

Now addressing Marco, "It was so wonderful to meet Cosimo. You both have been so kind."

Marco was visibly relieved. "I am sorry I had to leave the room but when I came back the machine was beeping and you were gone."

"No, I am sorry," I replied. "That was very rude of me. Thank you for letting me meet your father." My voice caught on the last word and tears started streaming down my cheeks.

"Please stay for lunch," Marco said, trying to change the subject. "It is ready."

My first instinct was to refuse the generous offer, especially since I was pretty sure Marco knew I lied to get in here. I didn't think he knew the real reason, but he was smart enough to know I wasn't representing a winery from America. I should have refused, but I couldn't leave.

"Thank you," I replied.

Pleased with my answer, Marco smiled and returned into the residence. With Antonio's arm around me, we followed Marco. I knew Antonio was anxiously waiting to ask me all about my time alone with Cosimo, but now was not the time or place. I just squeezed his hand and smiled to assure him that it had turned out as well as could be expected.

Marco led us down the hallway to a room at the back of the residence. This was even more grand than the first couple of rooms I had already seen. This being Antonio's first time inside, his head was looking from right to left the whole walk down the long, gilded hallway.

We stopped inside a room with a very long table in the middle. There were enough seating for a dozen people, but there were only place settings for three. Antonio and I were both admiring the portraits that adorned the walls and the intricate details of the tapestries. It was gorgeous.

"Come, sit." Marco gestured to the seats opposite his. There were men in black uniforms ready to pull out our chairs.

We sat and continued looking at the table, ceiling and each other. I was sure Antonio was wondering what I had gotten him into. So was I.

I never knew that the two little dots in Italy that showed up on my ancestry family tree would represented this. C.D.V. and Marco were just abstract notions to me only a few months ago. Not anymore.

Now they were real, very real. I could see, hear and touch them. The thought brought me back to Cosimo and holding his hand. We had made a connection and I felt it. My father knew who I was and he obviously did for the last twenty-two years. Why did no one tell me?

The servant poured water into our glasses first, and then wine in another. I noticed the bottle instantly. The moon. Did Marco suspect? I didn't think so.

Beef, fish and pasta was served. Vegetables from the garden looked delicious. I couldn't eat any of it. The knots in my stomach were gone, but they were replaced with butterflies the size of pigeons. I sipped my wine but knew I had to eat something. I forced myself to eat bites of pasta, carrots and bread.

I observed Marco as I ate. Antonio did, too. I was still very curious about my half-brother.

"Marco, did you grow up here, in this home?" I asked.

Marco, always with proper manners, finished chewing his food, laid down his fork and then looked up at me. "Most of the time, yes."

"Where is your mother?" I asked. I wasn't sure if this was rude of me or none of my business, but it did seem odd that he was alone with an ailing father. Antonio kicked me under the table.

Marco didn't let on if the question upset him, he simply answered, "They are divorced."

"Oh, I'm sorry," I replied. "I didn't know."

"It's fine," Marco said. "At least the fighting has stopped. It happened many years ago, I don't think they were very compatible."

"Do you see your mother?" I asked. Again, another kick under the table.

"Yes, I spent time at both residences growing up," Marco replied. "She is happier now. She married again and has more children."

Marco didn't realize that he had another sibling sitting right across from him. When I looked down at my plate I was surprised to see that I had eaten everything. I was feeling better and a bit more relaxed. Sitting with Marco was nice.

Desserts and more wine were brought out. The tiramisu melted in my mouth. The atmosphere was light and more casual. Even Antonio sat back in his chair and asked Marco a few question about the vineyard. I sat back and just listened. I had the answers I needed, or at least all that I was going to get.

I didn't know if Marco saw our resemblance, but I did. The same narrow face and dark hair. The nose, chin, even the shape of our eyes were similar. At one point we caught each other's gaze during dessert. We held that gaze as if we were each searching for something. In the end, we both just smiled and finished our food.

When lunch was over, Marco said that he had arranged a tour of the vineyard, "For your research," he added. Again, I felt guilty, but not as much. There was a golf cart type vehicle waiting for us at the bottom of the front entrance stairs.

I turned to Marco, "You're not coming?"

"No, I'm sorry," he replied. "I must stay with my father. You go and enjoy the tour."

Marco returned into the grand residence. We turned to the driver who tipped his hat and gestured for us to get in. It was amazing to see the rows of grapes as far as the eye could see. The driver took us down paved roads and then bumpy lanes that wound around the property.

The tour ended with a tour of the facility where the wine was kept. We sampled more varieties and saw where they stored their immense collection of bottles. Antonio, having grown up around here and owned a restaurant, was most impressed and asked lots of questions. I just took it all in.

I couldn't believe this was where Cosimo had been all of my life. I could have been here, too. Like Marco, I could have split my time between my mother and father. This was all denied to me. I was starting to feel sad and sorry for myself.

"I'm ready to go," I said, addressing both our tour guide and Antonio.

I started walking out towards our vehicle. Antonio helped our tour guide put the wine away. The emotions from the day were flooding through me all at once. The uncertainty, the pain, the joy and now the loss all ran their course.

I hugged my arms around me and cried. I was grateful that the men were not seeing me like this. I just needed a minute to get it out of my system. I walked to one of the vines and touched its leaves. They were so green and soft. The grapes weren't big enough to pick but they looked delicious.

I was saying goodbye to this place and the land. More importantly, I was saying goodbye to the people. I wouldn't see Marco again after today, or Cosimo.

I heard the men approaching and I returned to our vehicle that would take us to our own car. As we bumped back along the dirt trails and finally to the parking lot, I was glad I had come. Just like Chad had said, 'I would go'. I was very glad I did.

Even after our driver dropped us off and drove away, I found it very hard to leave. Antonio opened my car door, but I went over to the grand front steps and sat down. Antonio closed the door and sat next to me.

"Are you okay?" He asked.

I took a deep breath. "Yes, I think so," I replied. "As much as I want to leave this place, I can't." I looked into Antonio's eyes. "Does that make any sense?"

He smiled. "Yes, of course." He put an arm around me. "As much as I would like to know what happened in there, it is none of my business."

I nodded. I knew he was curious. This sweet and beautiful man, who only met me a few days ago, had given up his day to drive me all the way out here on an errand he volunteered for. I took his hand in mine and held it. I think I was trying to absorb all the strength and courage I could from him. It would never be enough. I had to find my own.

I was pretty confident that no one cared that we were lingering on the front steps. I didn't believe that Marco was looking out some window and wondering why we weren't leaving. He would be by his father's side, checking for reasons his monitors had beeped more quickly than usual or why Cosimo was crying.

I knew.

I turned to Antonio, "I will tell you everything, later. Right now I just want to say my goodbyes to this place."

We sat on the concrete steps for what seemed like hours. The sun was getting lower, the breeze was picking up and I closed my eyes. I let my other senses take over. I could hear the birds calling to their mates. I could smell the sweetness of the grapes on their vines. I could feel the warm wind caressing my skin. I could even still taste the faint dryness of the red wine we sipped just minutes ago.

This was as close to heaven on earth that I could ever imagine. I opened my eyes to take one more memorable gaze out onto the property. Pictures would never capture the full beauty of Frascati, but they would have to do, it would be all that I had left of this place.

I appreciated Antonio for giving me this day. I wouldn't have wanted to be here completely alone. Even though I came to Italy by myself, I couldn't have handled today without Antonio. I looked up at him, his arm still around my shoulders and I kissed him. It wasn't full of passion, but it was on the lips.

He looked at me with surprise that turned to empathy. I hoped that I hadn't made a mistake and crossed a line I had drawn. I liked the kiss. I liked Antonio. After a few more minutes of taking it all in, I took a deep breath and stood up.

I felt stiff from sitting so long and stretched. Antonio stood beside me and waited for my direction. I took his hand in mine. "Let's go home," I said. "I have so much to tell you."

Chapter 17

I filled Antonio in during the long and winding ride home. It was good to tell someone. He seemed interested, but I couldn't be sure. I was just some American girl who was renting his apartment that he met a few days ago, but he knew the Vernetti's.

Antonio grew up drinking their wine and learning their names. For him it was like a visit to the Vatican to meet the Pope. Even though he never met Cosimo, he met Marco, the heir to the empire. I was just the daughter that nobody knew or cared about.

As I told Antonio all the details of my day inside the residence, he showed appropriate compassion when I talked about meeting my father. He took my hand and squeezed it. His hands were warm and soft. I squeezed back and he looked at me. His eyes told me he truly cared.

I had never met anyone like Antonio before and probably never will again. It was almost dusk when we returned to my rental apartment. He opened my door and we stood on the sidewalk.

"Are you hungry?" He asked.

"Yes, but I have food upstairs," I replied.

Antonio shook his head. "No, I know a place that serves excellent food."

I gave him a sideways glance, "Better than your restaurant?" I said, jokingly.

He laughed. "Yes," he answered. "Meet me here in thirty minutes, okay?"

"Okay," I said, suspiciously.

Antonio left and I went inside and opened the door to my second floor apartment. I didn't know what to expect or where we were going so I showered and changed into white pants and a green short sleeved shirt. I sprayed some perfume and went back downstairs.

He was standing on the sidewalk with a small bouquet of flowers. "For you," he said.

"Thank you," I replied, accepting them but still wondering where we were going. "Are we walking?"

Antonio laughed, "Yes." We turned and re-entered the apartment building, but rather than ascend to the second floor, he led me into a first floor apartment. "This is my father's home," he explained.

I stepped cautiously into the apartment, identical to the one I was staying in. It was arranged a little differently and had more pictures and decorations to look at. Antonio returned from the kitchen with a vase filled with water. He took the flowers from me and placed them in the center of the dining table.

I followed him and saw that there were two place settings with lit candles in between. He did all of this in thirty minutes?

"Where is your father?" I asked.

"He's working in the restaurant tonight," Antonio explained. "He likes to walk around and talk to the customers. He calls it work, but really he is just being social."

I followed his voice into the kitchen. He was cooking something on the stove and it smelled amazing. My stomach growled in anticipation. There was garlic and oregano in it, I was sure. He had wine chilling and two glasses on the table. I helped myself.

His father's apartment didn't have a balcony like mine that looked onto the street. Being on the first floor, his went out back to a small courtyard. There were rustic chairs and a few plants. As I got closer, I could see there were herbs and a few vegetable plants. It smelled wonderful as I touched the scented leaves.

Antonio joined me in the small courtyard with his own glass of wine. He touched glasses with mine and took a sip.

"I'm sorry, I didn't wait for you," I said, holding up my glass.

"It's okay," he replied. "I forgive you." He smiled when he said this. He knew the long and emotional day I had and he was very sweet about the whole thing.

"Thank you for doing this," I said.

"I'm happy to do it," Antonio replied. "I wanted to do it."

He came closer to me and I could tell he wanted to kiss me. I turned my head and backed away. He straightened and returned to the food on the stove. I felt bad, but I didn't want to give him the wrong impression, maybe I already had. At that moment I decided that this was the last I would see Antonio.

I had one more full day in Rome and I would spend it alone, just like the first day. He had already given up too many days for me, I wouldn't allow him to waste anymore time on me. What I think he intended to be a romantic dinner followed by something else, turned into a quiet and quick dinner.

The food was delicious, of course, but I didn't want to stay long. After dessert, I went to get my purse.

"Did I do something wrong?" He asked.

"No, Tony," I started. "I am afraid I am giving you the wrong impression. I don't want this to go any further."

He walked towards me, arms outstretched. "I care about you, a lot, Luna. I don't want you to go."

"I know, but that's exactly the reason why I must go," I replied. "I'm leaving in one day and we will never see each other again. It won't work. I will spend the rest of my time in Rome alone and leave the following day. I'm afraid this is goodbye."

Tony crossed the distance between us in two strides. He took me in his arms and kissed me. It was a passion he had been resisting since the moment he first saw me when I ordered pizza at his restaurant. I found myself no longer resisting his kiss. I wanted it, too.

His arms tightened around me and mine held him tight. His hands came up to my face, my hair and my back. I felt the muscles in his arms and his chest tight against my own. I was able to bring my arms to his chest and slowly push him away.

I started crying. This was a man I could love. It just wouldn't work. His life was here and mine was in Erie. Even as I thought about home, I cringed. What did I really have back at home? No job, no boyfriend and parents who have been lying to me my whole life. It suddenly didn't seem so welcoming, but it was home.

"I...can't...do...this," I said through sobs. I opened the door and ran up the stairs and into the safety of my rental apartment, his apartment. I was suddenly feeling very claustrophobic. I was also very exhausted. I showered and went right to sleep.

THE NEXT DAY I AWOKE with a renewed energy. Everything was behind me. It was my last day in Italy and I was going to enjoy myself. I ate breakfast in my apartment and packed a lunch with my remaining food. I had decided to spend the day in Vatican City. I would tour St. Peter's Basilica and the Vatican Museum.

I was proud of myself for taking the bus and finding my way alone. As I passed through the great wall that surrounded Vatican City, I immediately felt calmer. There was definitely a peacefulness here that I never felt anywhere else. The circle of saints felt welcoming as I stood in the center of it all. I walked around, admiring the carvings before getting in line to enter St. Peter's.

I was glad I was here alone. Inside St. Peter's Basilica, I knelt at a pew and prayed. I prayed for Cosimo and Marco, my family here in Italy. I prayed for my family at home and for Chad. I prayed for my friends in Mexico, that they would make it home safely. Then, I prayed for myself, that I would find peace and happiness. Lastly, I prayed for Antonio.

It was funny how my thoughts always went back to him. I walked around every corner of the Basilica and admired all of the art and paintings. Everywhere I looked was painted walls, ceilings and detailed tile work. I lit a candle and said another prayer.

Outside the wall, I walked to the Vatican Museum. I never tired of its endless rooms and passageways. Priceless works of art were around every corner. There were so many moments where I needed to sit down and just let myself absorb it all. I noticed the floors, the smells, the chatter of the other guests, it all added to the powerful atmosphere.

I had spent my whole morning inside St. Peter's Basilica, but I was spending my entire afternoon in the museum. I continued winding my way down long hallways filled with tapestries until we finally reached the ultimate destination.

When I first glimpsed the Sistine Chapel, I was amazed. It wasn't until I entered the great room and stood in the center and looked up that I felt in awe. There was no other word for it, I was speechless at the beauty and the detail. That one man painted all of this was unbelievable.

They said, 'no pictures' but how could I resist? There were so many people, I kept my phone at hip level and with my forward facing camera, I snapped away. I didn't care if they were crooked or that someone's elbow got in the way, I needed to remember this day forever.

I found a seat along the wall and just took it all in. Pictures did not do this room justice. Unless you've stood in this room, you would never notice the details that made it so special. First of all the height, I never knew it was so tall. Another thing was how the light filtered in through the stained glass. I sat in the Chapel as long as I could, reluctant to leave the hallowed room.

There was more to the tour, so I continued to walk through the rooms. There was an outdoor space where I discretely ate my lunch. It wasn't much, not enough to draw attention. It just gave me enough time to rest and appreciate the grounds.

When I finally took the spiral staircase to the exit of the museum, I stood on the sidewalk and looked back at the stone facade. As I walked back towards the river, I stopped and watched street performers and artists along the way.

I crossed the Tiber River and waited for my bus back to the apartment. I had a wonderful day and felt ready to return home. I had questions for my mother, but also information to share. I decided to text Chad and remind him about picking me up. I had messaged him and my friends a little while I was here, but not much in the last couple of days.

'Are you up?' I texted.

His reply was immediate, 'Hi, Luna. How are you?'

I gave him a very brief outline of my day and confirmed my arrival time. He said it was in his calendar and that he couldn't wait to see me. I let him know that I had a great time here, but I was ready to come back home.

The sun was setting on my walk from the bus stop to the apartment. I passed a small restaurant and checked out the menu. I wanted pizza one more time before I left tomorrow morning and I didn't want to eat at Tony's restaurant.

My white wine arrived first. I sipped the familiar wine and read the label, Vernetti Vineyards. I had ordered tuna pizza for the first time because it sounded good. It was!

I savored every bite and ate the whole thing. I declined dessert and walked the rest of the way back. Antonio must have spotted me from the sidewalk because as soon as I reached the front door of the apartment, he was beside me.

He was out of breath. "How are you?" He started but did not wait for my answer, "I've waited all day to apologize to you for last night. I am so sorry for doing that. I hate myself for ruining our friendship."

"You didn't ruin anything, Tony," I replied. "I just don't think a long distance relationship will work for us. I needed time to think and clear my head. I'm leaving tomorrow."

Tony ran his hand through his dark curly hair, looking black in the shadows of the building. "I know and I'm very sad. I really like you, Luna."

"I like you, too," I admitted. I could tell he was fighting every instinct and muscle in his body to not take me and kiss me right here on the street. I appreciated that he didn't.

"At least let me drive you to the airport."

I wanted to refuse but I also wanted a proper goodbye. "Okay, pick me up at nine," I said. Then added, "In a car."

Tony laughed and nodded then took my hand and kissed the back of it. He returned to his restaurant and I went inside to pack, and cry.

Chapter 18

Today I was leaving Italy. I was both sad and ready. I woke up early and cleaned the apartment. I had done my laundry last night and it was all packed up neatly. I wrote Antonio a 'thank you' note and placed it on the bedside table. He wouldn't be able to read it until I was long gone, maybe even halfway over the Atlantic Ocean, so it didn't matter.

I sat on the balcony one last time with my coffee. I would always remember this trip. Perhaps someday I could return under better circumstances, but for now, I was glad I came. I was getting texts from my friends. They were leaving Mexico today, too. Their flight was significantly shorter than mine, so they would get home first.

I was excited to hang out with them and exchange stories, I was sure they had just as many, if not more, than I did. I was also eager to see Chad. He hadn't mentioned his parents, of course, he never did willingly, so I was concerned how things were for him at home. My floor was available again, if he needed it.

I washed my coffee cup, locked up and carried my luggage downstairs. I replaced the key in the lockbox and saw Antonio waiting outside, with his car. He took my luggage and placed it in the trunk and opened my door.

"Buongiorno," he said as I sat down in the passenger's seat.

"Good morning," I replied when he started the car.

We drove in awkward silence for the first few minutes, then he asked about my day yesterday. I explained that I had a wonderful time in Vatican City and how it made me feel so peaceful. He said that he had been there many times. He even said that no matter how many times he visited, he had the same reaction every time.

"It was magical and mystical," I said.

"Many places in Italy are," he replied.

I thought about his answer, it was true. Frascati was definitely high on the list, but my experiences in Italy were limited. I couldn't imagine what it would be like to live here, to be able to explore all over the country any time I wanted.

I supposed it was like that in America, too. I could travel to all four corners of the continental United States and still not see it all. We were both silent, again, deep in our own thoughts.

I risked a quick glance at Tony. His eyes were set on the road ahead of us. There was a physical attraction that I felt for him. I also really liked spending time with him. Was it love, could it become love? I wasn't sure. It had all happened so fast. I did know I would miss him.

I started seeing signs for the airport and knew that we were getting close. My palms were getting sweaty and I wiped them on my traveling pants. It was the same outfit I arrived in.

When we arrived at the departures area, he quickly retrieved my luggage, came around the car and hugged me goodbye. It was warm and sincere. Then, he kissed me. It was not a short goodbye kiss, this was passionate and without apology. Afterwards, we waved goodbye and he was on his way.

Stunned, I turned and headed into the airport. I checked in, passed through security and waited at my gate. I could still feel his lips on mine and I closed my eyes. I didn't want to start crying in the airport. Instead, I walked over to one of the little shops and purchased a water and some snacks for the plane.

Antonio had my head spinning out of control. He would go home and read my note, but it didn't matter anymore. I would be thousands of miles away before he eventually read the words, 'I love you'.

I COULDN'T SLEEP THE whole flight home. I watched more movies and took out my book to read. I may have dozed off a couple of times, but woke up when we were served food and drinks. I had a white wine and wrote in my journal.

The man next to me looked like a tourist, but when he spoke to the flight attendants, he spoke in Italian. I imagined he was visiting the United States in search of his father. I hoped he would have better luck than I did. I had met a father who couldn't talk to me and met a man I could not have.

When the pilot finally announced our descent, I got nervous and anxious. I still didn't know when or how I was going to approach my mother about it all. I was now even questioning whether I even would. No, I had to have answers, but I would wait for the right time.

After crossing an ocean, connecting flights and countless hours in an airplane, I was finally back in Erie, Pennsylvania. Chad was waiting at baggage claim and ran to me when he saw me approaching. He lifted me up in a bear hug.

"Hi, my little moonbeam, I missed you so much," Chad said.

"I missed you, too." He put me down and kissed my cheek. The earth and moon, together again. It felt good.

The ride home was quiet, I had so many things to tell him but I promised to fill him in later. Right now I had to decompress and collect my thoughts. I asked about his parents, he didn't answer. He just looked at me and smiled. I knew not to push him.

"Are you hungry?" Chad asked.

"No, they fed me enough on the plane."

"Okay, I just wondered," he replied.

He pulled into his driveway, but carried my luggage to my door. Inside, he even carried it upstairs for me. I followed him. No one was home, they were working. He sat on my bed and was looking at his hands.

"I have something for you," I said.

He looked up and smiled. "You didn't have to get me anything."

"Yes, I did. You drove me there and back, plus you kept my secret," I replied. I dug into my suitcase and pulled out a little paper bag with Italian writing on it and handed it to him.

Chad's eyes widened when he pulled out a brown leather wallet. He smelled it and then opened it.

"It's not from a designer, but it's a real handmade wallet with Italian leather."

"I love it, thank you, Luna."

The next gift he pulled from the bag was a last minute purchase from the Vatican Museum gift shop. It was a rosary that was blessed by the Pope, himself.

"It's heavy," he said.

"That's because it's filled with blessings and prayers just for you," I answered.

He thanked me, again, and I almost thought I saw him tear up. I started to show him pictures on my phone when he finally asked me, "Did you meet him?"

I put my phone on the bed beside me and turned to face Chad. "Yes," I answered. I told him the whole story from the beginning. He took my hands and held them. He knew this was hard for me. I explained how I knew he recognized me, or at least knew it was me. Chad smiled.

The story just poured out of me and Chad patiently listened to all of it. I told him about all the places I had visited and even riding on the back of Antonio's scooter.

"Who's Antonio?" He asked.

I reminded him that he was the owner of the rental and that when I called him for help, he offered to take me around. It tried to keep it sounding light and innocent, but Chad's expression changed. I didn't talk about Antonio any further.

"I'm so glad I went, though," I said.

"I knew you would be," he answered. We looked at each other, still holding hands. I really missed this.

Bear was at my feet wagging his tail from the moment I walked in the door. "I'd better take him for a walk," I said.

"Okay, I'd better get back to work, too."

I hadn't noticed until now that he was wearing a shirt and tie. He had left work to get me. Outside, I waved Chad goodbye and took Bear for an extra long walk. It would do me good, too, after all of the hours I had spent on the airplane.

I was getting texts from my friends wanting to meet up. We made arrangements to get together in a few days and I was really looking forward to it. We were back to reality. I needed a job. My summer grace period was official over.

I would start looking for jobs later. I had too much emotional baggage to deal with. The last thing I needed was to break down, unintentionally, during a job interview. I needed to process everything first.

My mother was the first one home that evening. I felt nervous and awkward giving her a hug and making small talk. I had to be extra careful that I didn't slip up and mention Italy, not yet. She started asking about pictures or if I brought anything back, I said I did but I haven't unpacked, yet. I wouldn't be able to stall for very long.

I escaped to my room when I felt her watching me. I wanted to talk to her alone, but not here, not now. Dad could walk in at any minute and I didn't want him to hear. I wasn't even sure he knew anything about Cosimo and I wasn't going to be the one to tell him.

Safely in my room, I opened my computer. I scanned through my emails to see if I had some miraculous job opportunity waiting for me, there wasn't. There were dozens of junk emails, though. I was deleting them so quickly I almost missed one from Antonio.

I froze. He had to have seen my note by now. Was there someone else renting the apartment today? I didn't open the email, I wasn't ready for what he had to say in reply to my note. Instead, I focused my attention on my luggage.

I started unpacking and putting clothes away. It was a simple task that kept my mind occupied. I put each item of clothing in my closet, then shoes and then toiletries. I finished writing in my journal and slipped it into the drawer of my bedside table. Those were memories to be revisited later.

Dad popped his head in when he got home. I gave him a hug and said I had a great time in Mexico. The fact that I didn't have a tan didn't even raise eyebrows because I never tanned. He was glad to see me home, he missed me.

I took my shower and it felt good after such a long day. It was funny to think the last shower I had taken was in the apartment in Rome. It was starting to feel like years ago instead of yesterday. My thoughts went to Antonio's email.

I opened my laptop and saw the unopened message. I stared at it for a long time before summoning the courage to click on it. What would Antonio say in response to my note? There was only one way to find out.

"Dear Luna,
I see my empty apartment and I miss you.
I read your letter.
I love you, too.
Ciao,
Antonio"

I slammed my laptop shut.

Chapter 19

I could not sleep last night. Maybe it was jet lag, maybe it was the message from Antonio. Either way, I was exhausted. I looked at my computer and remembered everything. Maybe if I just ignored it, it would go away.

I went downstairs to get some coffee. I was surprised to see mom making pancakes, until I remembered it was Saturday, both of my parents would be home. Mom asked how I slept and I said terribly. I couldn't even mention jet lag because a flight from Cancun wouldn't cause it. I was limited in my reasons.

"Mom, I have some bad news," I said.

She looked at me with concern. "What is it, Luna?"

"I didn't get into the master's program in Pittsburgh. Nancy did. I said I would still help her move down, though," I replied. I didn't know if this would be enough reason to make me so moody, but at least this was the truth. This was something real we could discuss.

"Oh, Luna, I'm so sorry," Mom said. "What will you do now?"

"I guess look for a job."

She nodded her head and went back to making pancakes. She offered me a plateful and I gladly accepted. We didn't talk any more until dad came down to eat. He kissed his wife and poured a cup of coffee. We all sat at the table and made small talk.

"I'm going out fishing today," dad said. "Who else wants to come?"

We all looked at each other and started laughing.

"I think you're on your own," Mom replied.

He wasn't expecting anyone else to come along, he never did. I think he enjoyed the peace and quiet the lake provided. He said goodbye and out he went. Alice was already at work, so it just left me and mom at home.

Mom was collecting the dirty dishes and wiping up the counter top. My hands were getting sweaty and my heart felt like it was going to jump out of my chest. It was now or never, we had the house to ourselves for several hours.

"Mom," I said. She turned to look at me, oblivious to the bomb I was about to drop. "When I got my passport, I saw my birth certificate." I watched her face for any hint of where I was going with this conversation. "There was another man listed as my father."

There it was, the first signs of acknowledgment. Mom blinked rapidly and pulled a chair out to sit down. She rubbed her face, but remained quiet. She wasn't saying anything, so I continued.

"Who is he?" I asked. This time I would remain quiet until she provided some answers. The cat was out of the bag. She needed to start talking. She did.

"His name is Cosimo Dante Vernetti and I met him in Italy," Mom said quietly.

"Does dad know?"

"Some of it, not the whole story," she said.

"What's the whole story, Mom?" I asked.

"I was young, younger than you. I took a trip to Europe with a friend," Mom started. I could tell she was reluctant to relive the details, but I wasn't going to leave without knowing the truth, finally.

Mom continued, "We were traveling all around for about two months. It was while we were in Italy that I met Cosimo." She smiled at the memory. "We were in a bar and we started talking. He was cute, a little older and exciting. He and I spent the next week together. I think my friend met someone, too, so she didn't mind."

I looked at my mom and tried to imagine her being in love with a strange man in another country, it didn't require much stretch of the imagination. I understood better than she knew.

"It was nice while it lasted," she said, interrupting my own thoughts. "I knew it wouldn't last. Anyway, I came home and found out a month or so later that I was pregnant. My parents were so upset, they told me to get out if I was going to keep it. I didn't know what to do."

Mom was playing with the napkin on table, folding it and refolding it. The pain of the memory was visible in her face.

"I called Cosimo to tell him and he sounded happy about it. I thought that meant we could be together, so I flew back to Italy. I know it was probably stupid and naive of me, but I thought we could get married. I had to see him face to face."

As I listened to her story I was surprised that she never told me any of this. Which parts did dad know? Did he know she wanted to marry Cosimo?

"I went to his house. I had the address but I had never been there before. It was large. There were men who came to the door instead of Cosimo and wouldn't let me in. I was crying on the front steps, but they wouldn't let me talk to him."

I knew the house, I also cried on those same front steps. I started feeling sorry for my mother.

"I went back to my hotel and it wasn't long until I had a knock on my door. I was so excited, I thought Cosimo had come to see me, but it wasn't. A couple of men walked in my room followed by two more. The first two were his family, I didn't know who, maybe uncles or even his father. The other two were their security personnel."

"Mafia?" I asked, not knowing where this story was going.

Mom laughed, "I really don't know, maybe, looking back. I felt so stupid. I was sitting in a hotel room, pregnant with four big men telling me to leave Cosimo alone. They wouldn't allow his future and his reputation to be destroyed by some American girl who wanted to trap him for money."

I could tell mom was having a hard time reliving the memory. She stood up to get a glass of water. She took a long sip and sat back down. Her story wasn't finished.

"Did you want money?" I asked.

"I never once mentioned money. I loved Cosimo and was having his baby. But, they seemed powerful. I didn't know anything about his family or what they were capable of. When I was with Cosimo, we always met at my hotel or somewhere else. His uncles offered me a lot of money to leave him alone."

This time she looked at me. "I didn't take it, though, not one penny of their money. I wasn't trying to trap him and I didn't want his money." She was starting to get more emotional and touched the napkin to the corner of her eyes.

"It was all so upsetting. They wouldn't leave until I signed a paper saying I wouldn't come back again. I signed it, but what hurt the most, and what really made me stay away and never look back wasn't the threats they made to me, it was what they said when they left."

"What did they say?" I asked.

"He's married."

My mother got up to refill her glass of water before continuing, "I felt as though all the wind was kicked out of me. I started hyperventilating and almost fainted right there in front of those men, but I didn't. With all of the strength and dignity that I could muster, I simply thanked them and asked them to leave."

"I never contacted Cosimo again until you were born. He tried to contact me, but I resisted. After you were born, I let him know your name and sent him pictures. I don't know if he ever got them. He seemed happy about you, though. It just wasn't meant to be."

"So, how much does dad know?" I asked.

"He knows Cosimo is the father, nothing about the threats. When you were born, I moved in with a friend and then started working. I worked at the diner right next to Ron's insurance agency. He would come in all the time and we started dating and that was that."

She stood up like that was the end of the story. It wasn't. I hadn't even told her my story, yet. I waited until she seemed to relax again before I told her where I really went on vacation.

"Mom, I didn't go to Mexico with my friends," I said. She looked at me and I knew she was confused. "I went to Italy."

"You what?"

"I looked up the name on my birth certificate and I went to Italy to meet him."

Her face went from confusion to anger, "Why would you do such a thing without discussing it with me first?"

"Because I wanted to meet him," I replied. "Regardless of what you would have said, I would still have wanted to meet him. I just didn't want you to be hurt or upset and cloud my opinion of him, so I went with an open mind and met him."

"You met him?" Her eyes were wide with concern.

I told my mother my story from the beginning. She was hanging on every word. I told her I was at his house, the one she was never invited in. I even told her about Marco. She was happy, sad, relieved and also worried that we would be hearing from his family. I told her that I didn't think so. There weren't any big scary men, only teenaged Marco.

She wasn't so easily convinced. "Don't contact them anymore. Let this be the last of the Vernetti's in our life."

I told her I had no intention of going back or contacting them. I had the only answer that mattered. He knew I existed and mom was probably his true love, although we may never know that part for sure.

"Anyway, he's dying. If there were any family trying to keep him away from us, I don't think they are as concerned anymore." I reassured her.

She nodded, but I don't think she was completely convinced. A living daughter of Cosimo Vernetti could still be a threat to the family, but they had already met me, how could I be trouble?

We couldn't believe that we had been sitting in the same place when my father came home. "Are you girls still eating pancakes?" He joked. It was four hours later.

"What did you catch?" Mom asked him.

"Oh, the usual," Dad said. "They were so big, I couldn't carry them, so I just threw them back in."

It was the same lame joke he's been telling for years. We laughed and rolled our eyes. We told him that we were just catching up, that's why we were still sitting in the same place he left us. I gave my parents a hug and went to take Bear for a walk.

I was about four blocks away when I got a text, 'Are you up?'

Very funny, Chad, it was only two o'clock, although I was very sleepy. 'What's up?'

'I heard about another great restaurant,' he texted. 'Do you like Italian?'

Well, he had jokes today. 'Nope!' I replied.

'But seriously, I have a new place,' he said.

I told him I would go eat with him, but probably not tonight. I really was tired and needed a good night's sleep. I would talk to him tomorrow and we could discuss it.

'By the way, I'm using both of my gifts,' Chad said.

The leather wallet and the rosary, one gift was practical but the other one was necessary. I had an idea what he was praying about, but all I could do was pray with him. That's exactly what I did before falling into a deep sleep that night.

Chapter 20

During the next days and weeks, I put all of my effort into finding a job. I was filling out applications daily. It didn't even have to require a marketing degree, I was open and willing for any reasonable position that would pay me a decent salary. It wasn't easy, though.

Friends and family were suggesting jobs and openings that they heard about. I was even getting texts about signs posted in windows. I wasn't that desperate, yet. I wanted to work somewhere that was interesting and not a place that was quick to hire high school kids. It was a difficult balance, apparently.

I had gotten together with my friends a few days after getting home. We all met up at the beach and swapped stories. They were shocked to hear all about my adventures and disappointed when I told them nothing happened between me and Antonio. I had spent enough time questioning my decision about leaving him, I didn't need my friends to do it, too.

I was happy to change the subject and hear all about their Club Med Cancun vacation. They all said they met someone, even though Jenny already had someone, but it was all in fun and that was that. I kept asking them to give more details, but they insisted there was nothing more to tell. I wasn't so sure.

We all promised that we would never vacation separately again. I did miss these girls. I expressed my need for a job and they all had their opinions. Trish said they are always looking for more realtors, or a receptionist in the office. Nancy would be two hours away soon, so she was no help. Jenny was at the bottom of the ladder as it was, she couldn't help me.

I was sure I'd find something soon, I just didn't know what it would be. I also didn't know how long it would take to materialize. I tried to be patient, but we were now at the end of August.

I had also gotten together with Chad, again. He promised he had another great restaurant to try out, and it wasn't Italian. It was Mexican. Chad ordered a beer and I got a margarita. He wasn't being very talkative, so while we waited for our food I decided to ask the hard questions.

I took his hand and asked, "Chad, how are you?"

He tried to shrug it off like everything was fine, but I knew better. "I'm good."

"How are things at home?"

"Good."

I knew things were bad when he said they were good. He also knew I wouldn't give up.

"I really want to ask Doreen out, but I know it will also be a waste of time," he said.

"Doreen?"

"Yes, the new teller at my bank," he clarified.

Now I remembered. She started a month or so ago. The last I knew, he said she was kinda cute. I also knew that dating a girl meant bringing her home and meeting his family.

Chad was stuck. He wanted to move out and live the life of a normal twenty-three year old, but he was afraid to leave his parents alone. If anything happened to his mother, he would never forgive himself.

I told him to go for it, maybe she is the one. Maybe she could look past all the chaos and violence that the other girls couldn't. I doubted it, but I didn't tell that to Chad. If I dated a guy who had such a violent home life, I would be afraid he would be the same way with me.

Chad was nothing like his father, he made sure of it. You wouldn't think such a big, tall guy would be such a teddy bear, but he was. He was stable, honest and loyal. He was also the earth to my moon.

"Well, if there's anything I can do to help, just let me know," I offered.

Our food arrived and smelled delicious. Chad got seafood fajitas and I got a steak burrito. After munching on chips and salsa, I was ready for the main course. I sampled Chad's and he tasted mine. I agreed this was a restaurant to keep on the list.

I felt the mood lighten while we ate. It was good that he talked about his concerns and I was happy to listen. Just a couple of friends with doomed relationships having dinner together.

IT WASN'T UNTIL SEPTEMBER that I finally had interviews lined up. I was so excited to finally be moving forward, not sitting stagnant in one place anymore. I had to drive all over the city and county for interviews, but that was okay. I had no idea which company might be willing to hire me, so I was willing to go the extra mile, literally.

The waiting was the hardest part. I got lots of rejections but I kept on submitting applications. I was starting to get very discouraged when weeks would go by without anyone willing to hire me, until I finally got an offer.

There was a new restaurant opening up downtown and they were doing okay, but wanted someone to help with the marketing aspect of the business. Their starting salary was at the lower end of my asking pay, but I was willing to give it a try if they were.

I started my new job in October. I had an office above the restaurant, but could work from home if I needed to. For now, I liked driving downtown and walking into my own office. I finally felt important, even if I wasn't.

I was able to invite Chad and even Trish over for lunches when they were available because they both worked nearby, too. It was nice to have the distraction. I was putting Italy, Cosimo and Antonio behind me.

It was during lunch with Trish when she brought up going on another trip. The fall was nice in Erie, but winter was coming. That was more than enough reason to want to get out of town and head to warmer climates.

I said I would think about it. I was working now and wanted to save money to get my own place. I had spent a lot on my trip to Italy, so I wasn't sure when I would have extra money again. Trish was doing well as a real estate agent. She said she would keep an eye out for a place for me.

Things were finally falling in line for me. It took nearly five months, but I was feeling optimistic. I had a job with a routine and I enjoyed it. The restaurant was doing better each week and they were happy with those results.

It started snowing one day at the beginning of November and never stopped. We now had a foot of snow on the ground, but the streets were solid ice. I considered working from home until we got a break in the snow, but I didn't think it was quite bad enough for that, yet.

As I walked to my car after work one night, I noticed that something didn't look right. It wasn't until I got closer that I realized a huge piece of ice had fallen from the roof and landed on my windshield. My first call was to my car repair shop to tow it away, the second call was to Chad.

'Are you up?' I asked. Our secret code for help.

'What's up?' He asked.

I explained my situation and he said he would swing by on his way home from work. As we drove home he insisted that I should ride with him to work each day until my car was fixed. I said I would get a rental, I was sure my car insurance would pay for it. He said that his suggestion would be way more fun. It was.

The auto repair said it would take at least a week. With the severe weather, trucks were delayed or not showing up at all so supplies were limited. I rode to work and home with Chad. It gave us time to check in with each other on a daily basis.

The weather was so bad that no one wanted to go out. The restaurant saw a drop in people wanting to dine in, but still had a solid delivery customer base. People were staying home but getting cabin fever. Even Bear didn't even want to walk in the cold and snow.

Things finally came to a head when one night, as Chad was turning the corner towards home, we saw six police cars in front of his house. The flashing red and blue lights were reflected in all the fresh white snow.

It took every once of self control for Chad to slowly drive on the icy road to his house. When he couldn't go any further because of the police cars, he ran out of the car and down the road. A policeman had to hold him back before they understood he was a member of the family.

I feared the worst as I got out of the car and slowly followed the path Chad had made in the knee deep snow. The wind was picking up and it was bitter cold. I could hear faint pieces of conversation as I made my way to Chad's side. Shooting, gun and arrested was all that I understood.

They were not letting him inside. I feared it was a crime scene, but I couldn't get any more information. I could see neighbors looking out of their windows at the commotion in the street, including at my house. Chad was becoming a handful for the officers and they were threatening to put him in handcuffs if he didn't settle down.

I stepped in front of him and spoke to him slowly. I asked him to go to my house and I would find out what happened. It was either that or he would be spending the night in jail. He looked at me and decided to go next door.

I pleaded with the officers to give me more details. I finally found one that was willing to tell me something.

"The husband had a gun and tried to shoot the wife. He missed, but the house is all shot up. He's been arrested for attempted murder. He has priors, so it doesn't look good for him," the officer said.

"Where is the wife?" I asked.

"They took her to Hamot Hospital to get checked out. But, like I said, she wasn't hit, just pretty shook up," the officer said.

I thanked him for the information and went home to relay the news. Chad immediately drove to Hamot Hospital. Well, this was the turning point for him. His father would likely spend his life behind bars. She was safe. He and his mother were free, in theory.

I just hoped Chad would see it that way. Would he want to move away and forget this place? Would he still feel obligated to take care of his mother? I knew he was still not in a good mental state right now, but I hoped he would find his way out soon. I would be here for him through it all.

I texted my boss and said I wouldn't be in due to a family emergency. I would be working from home for the foreseeable future. They were fine with that. According to my family, the police had been next door for hours. They had heard the gun shots.

Even Alice was so shaken up by what happened next door, she came over and gave me a hug. "How is Chad?" She asked.

"I don't know, Alice," I replied. "All we can do is pray."

I took a long, hot shower and climbed into bed. I reached for my phone when I heard a text come through.

'Are you up?'

'Chad, how is your mother?' I texted.

'She's good.'

'How are you?' I asked.

'I'm good.' He replied.

I knew it wasn't true. I wanted to reach through the phone and hold him and tell him everything will be all right. He just had to trust that it will be better now.

Another text, 'Thank you for tonight. I'd rather be sitting here in the hospital than in a jail cell.'

'You're welcome.'

I prayed for my earth until I fell into a deep sleep.

Chapter 21

It had finally stopped snowing which gave everyone a much needed break from the freezing temperatures. It was still cold, but above freezing. There was still snow on the ground, but there were also patches of grass showing. It was a perfect day to get out of the house.

I suggested several options for a family outing. It was too early to get a Christmas tree, too late to look at the fall foliage, but it was perfect for apple cider. We bundled up and drove about an hour out of the city. It was an apple orchard we had been going to for years. When the apples were ripe for picking, they would let you take a bushel basket and pick your own.

Standing in the middle of hundreds of apple trees with their ripe fruit was probably the sweetest smell I had ever experienced. Well, until I was standing in the middle of a thousand nearly ripe grapes in Frascati. I wasn't sure why that was still a fresh memory. It felt like a lifetime ago.

Today, we opted to purchase a bushel of apples already picked and two gallons of fresh cider. The store was filled with all sorts of apple products. They had apple cake, apple butter, apple ice cream and apple chips. We all sat down and had hot apple cider and cake. It was nice having something to smile about.

Even Alice enjoyed sampling all of the treats and ate a fresh apple. Alice was now a junior in high school and was already thinking about the prom. She would go with Evan, of course, but wanted to go prom dress shopping with me someday. I told her I would love to go with her.

We drove leisurely home, the scenic route dad always called it, with no hurry to be anywhere in particular. We were just enjoying the sunny day. When we pulled into the driveway, I noticed Chad just getting home as well.

My family went inside the house and I went over to Chad.

"How are you doing?" I asked.

"Good."

"How's your mom?"

Chad sat down on his front porch swing and I followed. "She's good. I helped get her all settled in and she looked happy."

After his dad was found guilty of attempted murder, and was sentenced to twenty years in prison, Chad's mom moved in with her sister's family in Pittsburgh. She was originally from Pittsburgh, so all of her family was still there. Chad was now the legal owner of the house next door.

"That's great," I replied.

We sat and just enjoyed being together. Now that I actually had a job that kept me busy, I didn't have all the free time I used to have. It felt good, the gravitational pull was still there.

"You know, it's strange, though," Chad said. "After all those years of wanting my own place, I never thought I'd be alone in my own house."

He didn't say it in a way that made me think he was sad about it, he said it matter-of-factly. I knew he had thrown away all of the things and furniture that evoked bad memories, which was nearly everything.

"Well, I like what you did with the place," I replied. "It's you." It was very much his style, minimal. It would take a woman's touch to make it a home, but for now it was perfect. Chad knocked down walls, repainted and remodeled the kitchen and bathrooms.

"You know," I said. "Trish could help you get top dollar for this place if you wanted to move away and start over."

"Now why would I want to leave the best neighbor in the world?" He replied with a smile. "Besides, Erie is home."

It was too cold to stay outside so when he went inside, I returned to my own home. I was eager to get my own place, too. I was still trying to save enough money so that I had enough cushion for all the other expenses that came with moving and setting up my own apartment.

I heard my phone ringing as I was cutting up one of our fresh apples.

"Hi, Jenny."

"Luna, clear your calendar for next Saturday! We are having Friendsgiving and everyone is going. Come to my house at two and we are doing another wine tour before our Friendsgiving dinner."

"Sure! That sounds fun," I replied, as if I had any other choice.

"Great," Jenny said. "This will be so fantastic!"

Making plans with my friends for another wine tour made me remember the last one we did. I had just found out that my dad was not my real dad. The news had been earth shattering, but I never discussed it with my dad. I don't know if my mom told him I knew, but I couldn't bring myself to say it. Ron was my dad.

The rest of the week remained mild. We didn't have any big snow fall and the sun melted much of what was on the ground. By the time next Saturday came around, it was gorgeous outside. That's just how things were in Erie in the winter, you could have blizzards one week and sun the next. Then it was dreary the rest of the time.

I drove to Jenny's house and was so excited to see all of my friends. They must have been waiting on me because as soon as I pulled up, they all came running out of the house. There were screams, cheers and hugs. I missed them. I never knew how much until they were right in front of me.

Nancy was on winter break from school, Trish said home sales were slower in the winter, but the sunny days helped a bit. Jenny was finally working inside the news studio instead of traveling all over the county. She still had high hopes for being on air soon.

There was never a lull in conversation the whole afternoon. I talked about my job and filled them in on Chad. Jenny dumped her boyfriend because he was too needy and everyone else, like me, just hadn't found the one, yet.

Each winery allowed old memories to resurface. I tried my hardest to hold them down, but they were strong. It was a struggle to stay involved in the animated conversations and participate in the stories. The wine helped.

We had visited three or four wineries by this point and had only eaten cheese and crackers in between. The wine was winning this battle. Jenny remained our designated driver and promised a full meal when we got back to her place. I was enjoying myself, until Nancy brought up Italy.

"So," Nancy started with a slight slur to her words. "Do you still talk to that guy? What was his name?"

Everyone was looking at me. I didn't want to answer.

"Antonio, wasn't it?" Trish asked.

"Yes," I answered. "And no, I don't keep in touch."

"Really? He never emails or texts you?" Jenny asked.

"I didn't say that. You asked if I kept in touch," I clarified. "He tries, I just don't reply."

Now everyone was looking at me with wide eyes and open mouths.

"You mean you have a hot Italian guy who wants to talk to you and you don't reply?" It was Nancy who asked but I know they were all thinking the same thing.

"Yes," I answered. "There is no point. There's no future for me there." I was hoping they would drop it, but I knew they wouldn't.

I didn't want to say what I was really feeling. I didn't want to admit out loud that I missed him.

"When was the last time he texted you?" Jenny asked.

"Two days ago," I replied quietly.

"WHAT?" They all said at once.

"You must reply now!" Trish said. "At least say hello or something. Give me your phone."

I refused to give anyone my phone, that was asking for trouble. However, between the wine, my friends' constant questions and demands, I gave in. I pulled out my phone and replied to Antonio's last text.

We were all sitting around Jenny's Friendsgiving table when the sound of a text message came through on my phone. All eyes were on me, again. They demanded to know what it said.

At first Antonio and I texted asking how each of us were doing. Then he said he missed me and thought about me everyday. He said he never rented his apartment out after I left because it didn't feel right. He wanted me to come back.

I would write and then delete endless responses to his text but then I finally decided on four simple words, 'I miss you, too'. My friends wanted me to write a whole Romeo and Juliet scene on my phone, but I wasn't that drunk.

In fact, I put my phone away and refused to look at it any more that night. I ate the delicious meal and tried to ignore the text notifications in my pocket.

I tried to change the subject by saying I wanted to get my own place. Trish and Jenny both said they were thinking the same thing. They suggested we find a house together. I wasn't sure that was the best route, but I said I would consider it.

I fought the urge to check my phone for the rest of the evening. Eventually, my friends gave up trying and we spent the rest of the evening eating pie and drinking spiked egg nog. It was dark by the time we all drove home.

At home, my thoughts went back to Antonio. Mom had made a whole kitchen full of Christmas cookies and I took a plateful to my room. It was wonderful hanging out and catching up with the girls. I don't know if I could handle being their roommate, though.

I couldn't take it any longer and read Antonio's text. 'Come back to me,' he said. It was impossible. Going back to Italy meant returning to the land of Cosimo and Marco. I couldn't do it. Even though Cosimo acknowledged who I was to him, he and his family treated my mother terribly.

There was no way to get more clarity from Cosimo, himself, so it was better to leave it alone and move on. That was exactly what I was trying to do here. I didn't respond to Antonio. Instead, I turned on tv and found a Christmas movie. Then, I started scrolling through apartment rentals in town.

I was determined to move forward. I wasn't going to dwell on the past or dig up old memories anymore. My friends meant well, but they didn't understand the whole situation. I couldn't go back to Italy.

The movie that was playing had turned too romantic for me and I changed the channel. It wasn't that I was anti-romance, just not tonight. I settled on Die Hard and continued to scroll through my phone, that's when I saw his next text message.

'I want to see you,' Antonio texted.

I wanted to see him, too. I wanted to ride behind him on his scooter, to feel his body against mine. I wanted to look into his eyes and kiss his lips, but I couldn't. I wasn't moving over there and he wasn't moving here. It was a dead end.

I didn't know what he expected me to do. I wasn't going to just fly over there and stay in his apartment to just sightsee. I wanted a career and freedom to do what I wanted. Right now I wanted to go to sleep.

I put my phone away, turned off the tv and went to sleep. I didn't want to think about anything else today. Antonio was part of my past.

Chapter 22

I was finally getting into the holiday spirit. With Thanksgiving right around the corner, I was ready for a few days off. We had plans to put up the Christmas tree the following week. This was my favorite time of the year.

Jenny called to let me know she found a house in the suburbs. There was an extra room if I wanted it. I thanked her and said I'd let her know. I wanted to move out, that was a given, I just wasn't sure I could handle Jenny full time.

Regardless of where I moved, I decided it was time to go through my room and get rid of things I didn't want anymore. I still had old school books that went into a donation pile along with some clothes and shoes.

By lunchtime, I had made a lot of progress and took things downstairs to load into my car. My mother was preparing dinner and was surprised to see me carrying boxes.

"Are you moving?" She asked.

"No, mom, just getting rid of some things," I replied. "I will, eventually, you know. Jenny even offered me a room."

Mom stopped what she was doing and came over to me. She said she knew this time would come eventually, but she would miss me. I would miss her, too. We had gotten closer over the last few months. More than we ever were before.

When she had finally told me the full story of her and my biological father, I really understood her pain. She had loved a man who ultimately rejected her because they couldn't be together. The Vernetti's must have been a very powerful family.

I didn't want to be part of their family, anyway. I was a Delaney and proud of it. My parents worked hard for what they had and we had a comfortable life. I didn't need anything more, except maybe my own place.

I texted Nancy to see if she wanted to meet up for coffee and she agreed. After dropping my things off for donation, I met her downtown. It had started snowing again but I didn't mind, it helped add to the holiday spirit.

State Street was lined with holiday lights on the electric poles. I could see the lake as I got closer to Perry Square. The lake was slowly freezing and it wouldn't be long before it was covered with tiny huts for ice fishing.

Nancy filled me in on everything happening at school and in Pittsburgh. She loved being in the big city, but missed her friends back home. She was studying biology and still wasn't sure if she would continue on for her doctorate. We had a nice conversation until she brought up Italy.

She had asked me about Antonio. I was tired of my friends bringing up the past. I said I never responded to his last message and wasn't planning to. I would not be going back and that was the end. She took the hint and we talked about Jenny's house and Trish's mom improving considerably.

Both were good news and worth celebrating. Jenny was planning on having a house warming party right before Christmas. I didn't think I would be moving in with her, but I wasn't going to make any major decisions right now. I wanted to enjoy the holidays at home.

When I got home, I took Bear for a walk. Now that we had snow again, Bear's walks were much shorter. He usually just wanted to do his business and get back in the warm house. I didn't blame him. I grabbed the mail before returning indoors.

I shook off the snow and hung up my coat. Dad was going through the mail and handed me an envelope.

"This one is for you," he said. The envelope he handed me was covered with a big yellow sticker from the post office. Apparently, whoever sent me the letter had written the address wrong and the post office had to correct it. It was post marked two weeks ago.

I dropped the unopened letter on the table and sat down. My parents turned to me with surprised looks. "What is it?" Dad asked.

"It's from Italy," I replied. I slowly opened the envelope. "It's from the law offices representing the estate of Mr. Cosimo Dante Vernetti."

My first thought was that the family was coming after me or my mom. I had angered them by showing up at their door and crying on their stairs, just as my mother had done twenty-two years prior. They wanted to make sure I never came back again.

"He's dead," Mom said softly.

"Probably," replied Dad. "That's usually when the estate sends out letters. It's probably about a will."

Dad was right. It was not a letter threatening me or my family. There was a lot of legal jargon, but I understood the gist of the letter. Cosimo died earlier this month and I was requested at the reading of the will.

"Do you think you're in his will?" Mom asked.

I had no idea. I was shocked. I had spent the last four months trying to put Italy behind me. All the reminders and messages were to be left unopened and forgotten. I froze when I saw the date.

"Mom," I said. "The reading of the will is in four days!" I looked again at the envelope and the wrong address. The letter was dated two weeks ago and I was just now receiving it. My palms were getting sweaty and I had a huge knot in my stomach.

"I have to go back to Italy," I said quietly. "Tomorrow."

IN MY ROOM, I WAS A hurricane causing massive destruction. I found my luggage and started throwing things inside and then taking them back out. My indecision was not letting me make any progress. I wiped my palms on my sweatpants when I realized I needed to send a text to Antonio.

'Hello,' I started. 'Cosimo has died and I must return to Frascati. Can I stay at your apartment? I will arrive the day after tomorrow.'

Antonio texted back immediately, 'Perfect!'

I didn't have the energy to explain that this had nothing to do with him. It would be an awkward reunion, but I did need his help. So, I guess it did have something to do with him. I could have gotten a hotel, but I chose to call Antonio.

My flight was leaving early tomorrow morning. I had to compose myself so that I could be productive but it was impossible to focus. I needed help.

'Are you up?' I texted.

Chad replied right away, 'Where are you?'

'My room,' I said.

'I'll be right over.'

I heard the chatter downstairs as my dad let Chad inside. Moments later he was entering my room. I showed him the letter and he looked at me with wide eyes.

"Wow!" He exclaimed. "When do you leave?"

"Early tomorrow morning," I replied. "Can you drop me off on your way to work?"

"Of course."

Chad was the calming effect I needed. He helped me focus on the clothes and shoes I needed for winter in Italy. I made my list of necessities and we checked them off as I packed each one. We were a good team and I wished he was coming with me.

"Are you going to see that guy?" He asked.

"Yes," I replied.

He didn't ask me any other questions other than when I would be returning. I said I didn't know. I got a ticket that I could change with no penalties because I had no idea what I was walking into. My heart started pounding again.

I sat down on the bed next to Chad. He could see I was having a mild panic attack and he hugged me. His embrace was exactly what I needed. Our cheeks touched and he was so warm.

"My little moonbeam," Chad whispered in my ear. "Just say the word and I will come with you."

I pulled away just enough to look into his eyes. "I have to go alone."

His hands slid down my arms and took my hands. "I know, but my offer is always open."

"I know," I replied. "Thank you for that."

"Especially if you tell me that Italian guy does anything to hurt you," Chad said.

I laughed and stood up. Being that close to Chad wasn't helping the situation, either. He crossed his arms in front of his chest and asked what was next on the list. After everything finally had a check mark next to it, I zipped up my suitcase.

I couldn't believe I finished packing. It was all thanks to Chad, the earth to my moon. As I went into the bathroom to collect a few last minute items, he had relaxed on my bed and turned on the tv.

"Make yourself at home, why don't you," I teased.

"Thanks," he replied with a sly smile. "It's just that living alone is so quiet. I never realized how comforting it was to hear someone in another room."

I stood looking at this twenty-four year old man who practically dominated my twin sized bed. Inside, he was still that scared little boy who wanted to be loved and protected, something he never got growing up.

I sat down on the fuzzy rug beside my bed and grabbed a bag of candy from my bedside table. I opened it, poured some in my hand and tossed him the rest. I moved next to him on my bed. We sat eating candy and watching a movie in silence.

It was the perfect way to spend the night before my unexpected journey. When the movie ended, Chad reluctantly returned to his house next door. I suddenly felt cold and put my robe on before heading downstairs.

Alice was in the kitchen eating some left over pie when I poured myself a glass of egg nog. Alice watched me carefully as we sat opposite each other.

"So, is it true we are only half-sisters?" Alice asked.

I almost choked on my egg nog. "Well, yes, it is."

I waited to see if she had any more questions. She didn't. I wasn't going to elaborate because I didn't know what my parents had already told her or not. It was probably best to just let this all play out organically.

Alice took her dish to the sink, hesitated a moment, but went back into the living room. I didn't know what she was thinking. Did our being only half-siblings make a big difference? Did it change anything? To me, it didn't.

I realized I hadn't even told my friends, yet. I had called my boss, but no one else. I decided to call Nancy and let her tell the others. I was tired of explaining it any more tonight. I had a long day ahead of me tomorrow.

Nancy was shocked, of course, to learn I was being summoned back to Italy. I confirmed that I would be seeing Antonio, again, but he was not the reason I was going back. It certainly didn't help the situation by staying at his apartment, but it would also be a good opportunity to end things for good.

I told her all about the letter and she hoped it would all be good news. I did, too. She asked if I needed a ride to the airport and I let her know that Chad already offered. There was nothing more to say. I didn't know when I would be back and that was a little frightening.

As I crawled into bed, I prayed that everything would be okay. I hoped that I would hear the will, would say goodbye to Tony and that I would be back in time for Jenny's housewarming party. In theory, it sounded like a solid plan.

Chapter 23

This time, the flight to Italy felt very different. I was no longer filled with excitement and adventure. I was feeling anxious because I didn't know how everyone was going to react to my appearance this time.

Marco will know that I lied about my identity to gain access to his father, our father. For such a powerful family, I didn't know how they were going to respond to that. They certainly wouldn't go through all of this trouble to arrest me, right?

How was Antonio going to greet me? I had literally ignored his messages for months. I only responded a couple of weeks ago and reacted coldly. Would he be just as cold to me when we reunited?

I was expecting the worst case scenario in every instance. At least my flight was pleasant enough. The seat next to me was empty and I was able to spread out and sleep. I could imagine I was flying anywhere in the world, until the pilot announced our descent.

My nerves took over and I was afraid to get off the plane. The flight attendant asked if everything was okay when I was nearly the last one to disembark the plane.

I could have gone into minute detail about how my life was falling apart right now and that I was walking into a black hole that was going to swallow me whole, but instead I just answered, "Perfect."

Every step I took through the Rome airport was filled with dread and fear. I managed to make my way through passport control and immigration without any problems. I found my luggage and exited the doors and what I saw next melted my heart.

Antonio was waiting for me with a dozen roses. I fell into his open arms and I immediately felt the stress from the last twenty-four hours leave my body. Antonio was here, he was happy to see me and we kissed.

It didn't matter that hundreds of people witnessed it or bumped into us. The spark and the passion was still there. He helped me with my luggage as he handed me the roses. Just like the flowers he gave me at his apartment when I first arrived.

On the car ride to the apartment, we both apologized to the other. He was sorry for texting me so much, he had no right to expect a reply. I was sorry for ignoring him and never replying. We were trying to act natural, but my heart was racing and I could see his breathing was shallow.

The sexual tension was obvious and mutual. I resisted him the last time I was here because I didn't think we had a future together. I still felt the same way, but would I still be able to resist?

At his apartment, he opened the door and I followed him inside. We didn't speak as he placed the roses in the vase on the dining table and I took my luggage to the bedroom. He had followed me. The look in Tony's eyes told me he didn't want to leave. I didn't want him to.

He took a step closer and he touched my face. I put my arms around his neck and we kissed. This was not like the kiss at the airport. There was no one watching. This kiss was a release of all the build up passion from last time. The last four months of waiting were gone in an instant.

He started unbuttoning his shirt and I took mine off, too. It didn't take long until we were in bed making love. We kissed and searched each other's bodies until we knew every inch. I shouldn't have ignored Tony for so long. This felt right. Maybe we could make this work after all.

Everything else about my day was forgotten in this moment. I didn't know where I was or what I was doing here, I just knew I was with Tony. Hours had gone by but it wasn't until his phone rang that we noticed the time. It was later than we thought.

"I am going to stay with my father while you're here," Tony said.

"Why?" I asked. After tonight, I didn't think I could be without him.

"Well, I didn't think this was going to happen," he replied, gesturing to the bed.

I laughed. Of course, Tony would be the gentleman and make arrangements for him to stay elsewhere. I appreciated him even more for that. No, it was deeper than that. I loved him. I think I never stopped loving him.

"I will allow you to stay here," I teased.

"You will allow me?" He asked. He kissed me again. "I love you," he said.

"I love you, too."

Later, Tony cooked a pasta dish for us and then I tried to get some real sleep before my big day tomorrow. My meeting with the lawyers was at ten o'clock and Tony said he was taking me. It would be nice to have him there. He had been on this journey with me and it wouldn't feel right without him beside me.

The next morning, the knot in my stomach returned. I chose to wear black wool pants, a red sweater and black boots. Even Tony dressed up, even though he didn't know how he fit into today.

My biggest concern was facing Marco. I lied to him and he could be furious. In August, I could have been there to get revenge on my father and he left us alone in the room. I didn't actually know how Cosimo died, that was never explained to me, but Tony said it was on the news.

"He was an important man," Tony had explained. "He was well known in Italy."

It was time to go. Ready or not, I had to face this. This time, the winding roads were making me nauseous. No longer an enjoyable day trip, I was getting more nervous with every mile we covered.

The address the lawyer provided was different then the one I had visited last time. As we turned off from the main road, we followed a long driveway lined on both sides with trees. They were bare this time of year, but I could image the impact the foliage would provide to visitors.

The house got larger as we approached. If I thought Cosimo's house was grand and opulent, it looked like a shack compared to this palace. The gravel driveway came to a circle in front of the house. There was a fountain in the middle of the circle with stone horses leaping out of the middle.

As we got out of the car, I looked up. The house had four stories with steps leading up to the front entrance and then opened up into a large veranda. There were manicured bushes all around the residence and in the gardens that were visible from the driveway.

Tony was also slowly coming around to my side of the car and we walked up the front steps together. There were large pots on both sides of the door that held evergreens. Our eyes both looked up to the lion-faced door knocker.

I swung the large metal ring and knocked twice. A butler answered and gestured for us to enter. Another appeared as the door closed to take our coats. A man was approaching from down the hall that I soon recognized to be Marco.

I couldn't read his expression. He looked older than his nineteen years, I suppose losing his father had made him grow up a bit more. Marco still had his hair cut short with only a few curls coming down the front.

I watched as he came to a stop right in front of me, still expressionless. I was ready to bolt out the front door at the slightest provocation. There was no need. Marco leaned in to give me an unexpected hug.

"I never knew!" Marco said. "My father never told me until recently that you were his daughter, my sister."

I didn't even realize I was holding my breath until I let it out. Marco was no longer expressionless. His eyes were searching mine for answers. He looked more closely at my hair, my nose and my chin. They should be very familiar to him.

Marco looked from me to Antonio. I introduced them to each other. They had met each other the last time I visited Frascati, but it seemed like Marco didn't remember him. Antonio, however, would never forget meeting someone from the famed Vernetti family.

"Please follow me," Marco said. "Everyone is ready."

Marco led Antonio to the library where he was to wait. Marco and I walked down more hallways filled with portraits, tapestries and gold vases. Marble floors were covered by delicately woven rugs that led us to a large room.

This room was larger than any room I had seen in Cosimo's house. There was a long table down the middle that could easily seat fifty people or diplomats. There were already a dozen people seated and all heads turned to me when Marco and I entered the room.

They all watched my every move as a man pulled out my chair and I sat down. I tucked a strand of hair behind my ear and cleared my throat. All under the scrutiny of other family members who probably never even knew I existed until only a few days before.

If I was scared before, I was entirely frightened at this moment. Marco sat beside me and nodded reassuringly. I smiled but my insides were in knots. I had no idea what this document would say and what I was even doing here.

The lawyer, at the head of the table, introduced himself and started to talk. He let the record state who all was present and more curious eyes fell to me when he said, 'Luna Gabriella Delaney'.

He started reading the will and there were some things I understood but most things I didn't. I used this time to observe everyone around the table. They couldn't be children, Marco was his only son. Most likely they were cousins, uncles, aunts or even siblings. They all wanted a piece of the fortune.

It was sad to think that the empire came down to names on a page. Perhaps I would get the golf cart, or a portrait on the wall of some distant relative. If it was something that would fit in my suitcase, that would be great. I still wasn't sure why I was even here.

As names were being read, the corresponding person was either visibly happy or upset. I didn't know what they were getting, maybe shares in the company or the silver tea set. It wasn't until I heard my name that I listened more closely.

"To Marco Vernetti and Luna Gabriella Delaney, being my sole surviving heirs, I leave them each fifty percent of Vernetti Vineyards to continue to run the company in my absence. Marco will receive my home where I have resided the last twenty-five years. Luna will receive the main house to own and reside in."

There was more, the lawyer was still talking and I was sure the gasps from this room were heard down the hall. All I could hear was my heart pounding in my ears. I looked at Marco and he was smiling at me. I could feel tears pooling up in the corner of my eyes.

What did I just hear? Fifty percent, with Marco? I thought I was talking but apparently no words were coming out. Marco's face changed from smiling to concern as he called a servant over with water.

I could feel all of the blood drain from my face, I was sure it had scared Marco. After drinking the glass of water in one gulp, I stood up and ran out of the room. I continued to run down the hall until I spotted Antonio.

Surprised to see me, he opened his arms and I fell into them, crying. Marco had followed me and stopped when he found me in the library.

Confused, Antonio asked Marco, "What happened? Did she get anything?"

Marco simply smiled and answered, "Yes."

"What did she get?" Antonio asked.

"Half of everything!"

Chapter 24

"I'm sorry I ran out of the meeting," I said to Marco.

I was embarrassed by what I had done in front of all those people. My shock was wearing off but I still wasn't sure what all of this meant for me. I thought that I might be dreaming.

Marco laughed. "Don't worry about them," he said, gesturing to the room at the end of the hallway. "We heard what we needed to hear."

"Which was what, exactly?" I asked.

"You and I, being our father's only children, will inherit this," Marco replied, again gesturing with his hands.

"This?" I asked.

Marco motioned to the seating area inside the library. We all sat down. Antonio was beside me and Marco sat in the chair opposite us. He explained that he was to live in his father's house, it was plenty of room for him. I was to live here, in the palace.

Maybe my eyes were glazing over, because Marco paused, then continued. We would run the winery together, all aspects of the business would be joint decisions. The other family members received certain items, positions or money, but only his children received the estate.

My head was spinning and I looked at Antonio. He looked impressed, I was sure that I looked like a deer in headlights. I start looking all around the room. It all belonged to me now.

"I know it's a lot to take in," Marco said. "You don't have to do anything right now. You don't even have to move to Frascati right away. In fact, we can buy your half if this is something you don't want. It's completely up to you, sister."

I looked at him as he said the last word. "I have something for you," Marco continued.

I couldn't believe he could give me anything more. I already had half of everything. As Marco stood up and left the room, I leaned on Antonio.

"Wow!" Was all he could say.

"Yes, wow!" I agreed.

Marco returned with a wooden box. It was about the size of a microwave and had intricate carvings and paintings all around it. As Marco set it on the table in front of me I saw the name carved on the top, Luna.

My eyes were welling up with tears and I brought my hand to my mouth. "That's me," I said.

Marco explained that his father had this box for as long as he could remember. It was on a table in his father's bedroom. It was always locked and he would never let him touch it or open it, ever.

There was also a carving of a moon that encircled my name. The same design that adorned every one of Vernetti Vineyard's bottles of wine. I touched the carvings as if they were made of bubbles that might burst. I ran my hand over the top and down the sides.

Marco explained that he did not know about me, but suspected there was a secret his father had been hiding. I told him the story my mother told me. I said that she long suspected that Cosimo was somehow connected to illegal activity, perhaps that could explain some of the secrecy.

He admitted that the family had done some bad things in the past, but it was our father who cleaned up the family name. He rejected all forms of behavior that he didn't want in the family. Cosimo had built a family empire to be proud of.

Marco said that after I left in August, Cosimo made a remarkable improvement. His doctor could take him off the ventilator and he was able to talk a little. He was sitting on a real chair and having full conversations. It was during this time that he told Marco all about me.

He relayed the tale of meeting Shirley and how she went back home to America to have the baby. Cosimo knew she couldn't come back to live with him because he was already married to Marco's mother. He didn't know about the visit to Shirley's hotel room or the money offered her.

Cosimo just knew that he was in an arranged marriage he didn't want and had a daughter in another country he could never see or acknowledge, the family would never have allowed that. When Marco was finally born, a few years later, he was hoping he could finally move on from it all. A few years later he divorced Marco's mother but by then, Shirley stopped all communication.

"Wait," I said. "They were communicating?"

Marco said this was where the box came in. Everything having to do with me was inside of it. Marco handed me the key. He hadn't even seen inside. He asked me if I wanted him to leave but I welcomed him to stay. There would be no more secrets in the family.

I took the key from Marco and opened the lock. It was like opening a real life treasure box. There were letters addressed to Cosimo in my mother's handwriting. There were numerous pictures of my mother pregnant, me as a baby and then as a toddler. They were wrinkled and smudged as if they were handled and looked at often.

There were also things that Cosimo, himself, had made or added to the box. One of these items looked like a desk plate that any business man would have on their desk. It was not your average desk plate, this one was hand carved, Luna Vernetti.

I rubbed my fingers over the carving of my name, a version of which I had never seen before. I could have been Luna Vernetti. On the very bottom of the box were little pink booties and tiny little foot prints pressed onto white paper that had yellowed with time.

I was feeling overwhelmed and closed the lid. I had seen enough for one day. I thanked Marco for his hospitality but I was ready to leave. We all stood up, our coats were brought to us and we exited the palace, my home.

I rode back to Antonio's apartment with the wooden box on my lap. It was my last connection to my father. Marco said that after Cosimo's period of improvement, he took a severe turn for the worse and never recovered. Marco was thankful for those last months with his father.

Marco believed that his improvement was a direct result of my visit. Marco had suspected that I wasn't really a representative from an American winery, but he never knew I could be his sister. His father happily admitted to everything and was thankful that I had come.

My hands traced the name, Luna, on the lid of the box. I was sure he carved it himself. Tony watched me out of the corner of his eye. I knew he saw me differently now, I even felt different.

"So, your highness, what would you like for dinner tonight?" He asked.

I punched his arm. "I'm not royalty," I protested.

"To Italian's, you are," Tony said.

I thought about that. Vernetti Vineyard was everywhere here. I knew what he meant, but what did it mean for me? Was I moving to Italy? It was a lot to think about and I certainly wasn't going to make any decisions tonight, except that I wanted pizza for dinner.

Tony put the wooden box inside his apartment and we walked next door to his restaurant. It was busy, but he found a table in the back. This was a table that was never given to customers, this table was reserved for family.

Tony brought two pizzas from the kitchen, one cheese and the other, tuna. I had told him how I fell in love with tuna pizza on my last day when I was here in August. We sipped Vernetti wine and ate pizza in silence. I had so much to think about.

I stared at the wine label, I was a Vernetti. I was sure that this would be big news in Italy, just as news of Cosimo's death was. There was an American heir to Vernetti Vineyards, me. Marco had said that the next time I came back, he would have his accountants go over all the financials with me. I had access to a bank account, now.

The more I thought about it all, the more I started to smile. I was letting the good news replace the fear. Tony watched the change in my expression.

"You look happy," Tony said.

"I am," I replied. "Cosimo didn't just acknowledge that I was his daughter, he acknowledged it publicly."

"He sure did!" He agreed. "Soon all of Italy will know who Luna Vernetti is."

Well, that didn't add any pressure! I hadn't seen any photographers, yet. I smiled when I thought of them trying to dig up a photo of me and ending up splashing some high school yearbook photo on all of the tabloids.

"I am glad you are happy," Tony said. "It was big news today and even I can't believe it. Your head must be exploding."

I nodded in agreement because it was a pretty accurate description. We finished our wine and pizza and returned to Tony's apartment. I didn't want to be alone tonight, so he stayed again. I decided not to go back to Frascati, not this trip. I didn't want to be persuaded by all of the gold and velvet.

If I decided to come back, it would be because I really wanted to be here and embrace this life. I wasn't ready to do that, I wasn't sure I ever would be. I called my parents to let them know I would be coming home the day after tomorrow. I wanted one more day with Antonio.

I texted Chad to let him know, too. I knew he was worried about me, but he didn't need to come and punch Tony in the face. I was excited to tell everyone the news, but also worried how my family would take it.

I didn't want mom, dad or even Alice to feel like I was choosing one family over the other, I could have both, couldn't I? We could all move to Italy and not have to worry about anything, or was that just in fairytales?

I was mentally and physically exhausted. Jet lag was only part of the reason. I showered, changed and crawled into bed. I pulled my little journal from my bag and started writing everything down. When Tony came to bed I had finished writing and put it away.

"Hold me," I said.

"Forever," he replied.

I felt the warmth of his body and the strength of his arms around me. I closed my eyes. I could still hear the faint sound of the television program that Tony watched as I drifted slowly to sleep. My dreams were starting to mix in with reality.

I thought about what it would be like to go to sleep in the palace. There would be bedrooms for my parents, Alice and even Chad. If Trish, Nancy and Jenny wanted to live with me, they could have rooms, too.

I imagined that everyone I loved were surrounding me in that big gold and velvet building. Tony was there, too. I didn't know what everyone was doing there, but they all looked happy and so did I.

I must have been dreaming, it couldn't be real. I was walking down a velvet covered stairway dressed in a blue ball gown and wearing a crown. I lost a glass slipper somewhere because I only had one shoe on. I ran down the long hallway lined with portraits of old people and opened the front doors.

Outside I tried to find my horse and carriage. I ran through rows of grape vines and couldn't find them anywhere. The only thing I saw at the front door was a pumpkin. I looked up to the sky and saw a full moon and made a wish.

I wished for a large wooden box filled with letters and pink booties.

Chapter 25

I woke up the next morning after a restless night. My dreams made me feel uneasy. I didn't know what they meant, but I was glad that it was morning. It took me a moment to remember where I was, then I looked at Tony laying beside me and it all came back to me in a flood.

"Buongiorno," he said.

"Good morning," I replied.

He kissed me and said he would go downstairs and get some food from the restaurant. I was glad for the space. I got dressed and made coffee. The large wooden box was sitting on the dining table. I had gone over the contents a dozen times and I still couldn't believe it.

Tony returned with fresh fruit and croissants, my first breakfast I ever ordered in Italy. He remembered. I sat on the balcony and ate my breakfast. The sounds of traffic, people and birds were comforting.

Even though my flight was tonight, Tony said he had the whole day planned.

"Italy is more than wine and ruins," he said. "I will show the real Italy."

"As long as you can show it to me in twelve hours or less," I replied.

He came over and kissed me. "I love you," he said.

"I love you, too."

I would miss Antonio when I went home. I wasn't afraid about a relationship anymore, but I was still skeptical that it would work. Resisting it was too much work. I had decided we could give it a try.

I packed up my things and Tony carried my luggage downstairs and into his car. I had still managed to write him a note that I knew he would see when he went to bed tonight, alone. This was a very short trip, but it felt like I had been here longer than just a couple of days.

Tony drove us an hour out of the city and the scenery was beautiful. Even in the cold months, Italy did not disappoint. We passed pastures, fields and small towns until he finally pulled into this little dirt driveway.

It was a farm with a large stone house. Not a grand house, but a decent size for a family. I could hear goats and sheep that were roaming around nearby on the property. Tony walked up to the front door and knocked.

"Do you know these people?" I asked.

"You could say that," he answered with a smile.

It took a minute for someone to come to the door. When it finally opened, a little old lady appeared. Her face lit up when she saw Tony.

"Buongiorno, Antonio!" The old woman said.

Tony spoke to the old woman only in Italian. He explained that I was his friend and she gestured for us to enter. I could see she had soup on the stove cooking and coffee ready on the kitchen counter.

"This is my grandmother," Tony explained.

She gave me a hug and told us to sit down. She poured us coffee and sat with us. Tony and his grandmother talked and laughed and I could feel the warmth of family here in this little kitchen. Tony said we would come back for lunch, but right now he wanted to show me the farm.

We walked down to the barn and met his grandfather, who was brushing a horse. My guess was that they were in their seventies. Tony said that he and his father came here and helped out when they could, but they were so busy themselves.

"When I was a kid, though," Tony said, "this was our playground." He gestured with both of his arms outstretched.

I couldn't imagine growing up with all of this land. Our backyard in Erie could maybe fit a swimming pool, but that was about it. This was acres as far as you could see. It wasn't grape vines, but it was still beautiful.

After helping his grandfather put the horse back into his stall, we walked out to see the goats. They came right up to us expecting food. When they didn't smell any, they went about their business.

We had walked a big circle on the property and were getting cold. Tony led us back to the main house for some soup. We each took our bowls of hot soup into the living room where his grandparents had a roaring fire in the fireplace.

There was a fresh cut Christmas tree in the corner filled with lights and decorations. It was cozy here. Tony said that after the overload of information yesterday, he wanted to show me another side of Italy. Not the hustle and bustle of the big city or the opulence of the palace, but there was a part of Italy that was in between.

I wouldn't be choosing one or the other, I could have every part of Italy. When the chaos of the big city got to be too much, he came here and changed horse shoes or fed the goats. It put everything into perspective.

I was starting to see his point. I didn't know if I could embrace a life of servants and velvet curtains, but if I had a normal life outside of that, then I just might keep my sanity. It was just one more thing for me to consider while making this big decision.

The soup was delicious. I could tell all of the vegetables were picked from her garden. Tony caught me looking at him and winked.

I could get used to this, with him. His grandparents came in to check on us and asked if we wanted any more.

Tony said that cake would be coming out of the oven in five more minutes. I smiled and watched the flames dance in the fireplace.

"Thank you for bringing me here," I said.

"You haven't even tasted her cake, yet," Tony replied.

We both laughed a very contented laugh. We did have some cake, hot from the oven and it was delicious. We stayed and visited a little while longer before we had to head towards the airport.

It was a lovely afternoon and I was glad that he had brought me here. I had considered spending my last day alone like I had done the first time, but I was going to have enough days without Tony in them, so I didn't want to waste any of them.

I enjoyed meeting Tony's family. I wanted him to meet mine, but I didn't see that happening. On the ride back into Rome, I looked for my journal in my backpack but I couldn't find it.

I told him that I thought I left my journal back at his apartment. I wrote down my address so he could mail it to me in Erie. He said he would. I hated that I left it behind, but I would just have to write in it when he sent it to me.

The ride to the airport took a couple of hours. I found myself dozing off at times. This time I would definitely miss Italy and Tony, but the chances of my coming back to visit where much greater than they were in August.

Back in August, I didn't believe I would ever come back. I didn't want to. Now, everything has changed, for the better. I now had people who were really waiting for me to return and that felt good.

I also had people waiting for me back home and that felt good, too. I couldn't wait to tell everyone what happened. I left the wooden box at Tony's apartment. It belonged in Italy and I would see it again if I returned.

We stopped at a small restaurant along the way. Tony ordered for us and I was grateful for the help. We sipped our Vernetti wine and waited for our meals. It was these quiet moments that I would miss the most. Just he and I sitting at a small table looking into each other's eyes.

He fell in love with me when I was just a crazy American girl on a mission to meet a man. I fell in love with him because he was kind and knew how to cook. Now we knew more about each other than we could ever imagine and it felt good.

Our pasta carbonara arrived and it smelled and tasted wonderful. I savored my last meal in Italy. I didn't know for sure if or when I would be back, that was the hard part.

I had been telling Tony that we would try and make this work, but I honestly didn't know how. Was I fooling myself into thinking I was really coming back to Italy? Even Marco said I didn't have to.

We finished our meal and got back on the road. We were both pretty quiet the rest of the way to the airport. When he finally dropped me off he gave me a long hug and then we kissed. It was not a deep passionate kiss. It was a kiss that said, 'Come back to me'.

I passed through security and then bought a water, some snacks and a book. I didn't want to think about anything the whole flight home and hoped to get lost in a good book. I settled into my window seat and let the world melt away.

I should have known it wouldn't be that easy. I read for a little while, then tried to watch some movies. It was no use, I missed Tony and I was not looking forward to going home. I would just have to give myself time to readjust to life without Tony.

I wouldn't make any rash decisions until I had discussed it with everyone, especially Chad, his was the one opinion I could count on the most. The thought of him was the one thing that made me ache for home. The thought of leaving Chad behind was unimaginable.

The pilot announcing our arrival into Erie International Airport was probably the best thing I could have heard right now. I grabbed my bag from the carousel and went to see Chad. He was waiting for me right where he was last time.

The rush of emotions were catching up to me and I ran into his arms in tears. He held me for as long as I needed and then took my suitcase to his car. I felt complete, again. He was just as happy to see me as I was to see him.

It was dark outside, so it was easy to see all of the Christmas lights on the drive home. I asked how he was doing and he said he was good. He asked about my trip and I said I would tell everyone my story tomorrow. Right now I wanted to enjoy being home. I would think about Italy tomorrow.

Chad knew that I would talk when I was ready, just like him. I wanted him to know everything, but it could wait. Right now I just wanted to enjoy this moment of gravity between the earth and moon.

He pulled into his driveway and carried my luggage to my door. I thanked him again and waved goodnight. Mom was at the door and opened it wide for me to enter. Bear was there with his tail wagging. Dad and Alice were watching football on tv.

I knew they were full of questions but I appreciated the fact that they didn't bombard me with them tonight. I had already talked and texted the main points and the rest would be filled in tomorrow.

For now, they let me go to my room and shut the door. I texted Tony to let him know I made it home safely. The next thing I remember was showering before I curled up in bed and fell into a deep sleep.

This time there were no big blue dresses or glass slippers. There weren't even grapes or pumpkins. This dream was of the earth, moon and goats, lots of goats.

Chapter 26

The next morning, as I walked past my unopened luggage, now an obstacle on the floor, I knew I didn't want to go back to Italy. Outside, the snow was falling in small snowflakes that flew in the wind before hitting the ground. This was home.

I could hear Christmas music playing from downstairs and knew that meant my parents were both up. It was only a week until Christmas, so there were still more preparations to be made. I also knew they were waiting for me. Today I had to explain everything.

'Are you up?' I texted.

'What's up?' Chad texted back.

'Can you come over?'

Chad was knocking on the door ten minutes later. I decided that if I was going to keep telling the story, I may as well get as many people together at once as possible. This was my family and it affected them almost as much as it did me.

We all had some of mom's freshly baked banana muffins and coffee and then eventually transitioned to the living room. I shifted in my seat as all eyes were on me. As I looked into all of their faces, I knew this was all going to be a shock to them. They had no idea what was coming.

I first explained how I had sent a bogus email to Marco in order to get invited to see him and Cosimo. What I didn't know was that Cosimo had recently suffered a stroke and couldn't talk, move or get out of bed. I explained how I knew he acknowledged me as his daughter.

Mom was starting to get emotional. Whether the tears were for her, Cosimo or me, I didn't ask. Dad just rubbed her back and smiled. I continued.

I also talked about Antonio. He was now a significant part of the story, so I made sure to mention that I met him on my first trip over there in August, too. This was all a precursor to the main event. I was getting everyone up to speed right until I got the letter summoning me to Italy.

Now we were at the good part, or the bad part, depending on the perspective. My palms were getting sweaty and I took a deep breath. I focused on Chad.

I described my visit to the larger home, the palace. How I was sitting in a room full of Cosimo's family and then ran out. I inherited half of everything, I said slowly. The full impact of this sentence didn't quite hit them because they weren't there. This was the part for visual aides.

I opened my laptop and scrolled through the photos. They saw the vineyard, the front steps to the residence, the hallways and the rooms. I included photos of Marco and Antonio. Chad's face changed into a scowl, but I continued.

I showed every picture I had of the Vernetti estate. When I finished, I felt they had a better understanding of the magnitude of change this earthquake had created. The impact of which could be felt right here in this living room.

They all sat back and asked to see the photos, again. Even Alice, who had been quiet and seemingly unfazed by the whole presentation asked the first question.

"Are you moving there?" Alice asked.

All eyes were back on me. It was the one question that had been going through my mind since the moment I heard the will being read. I had thought of the pros and cons of each possibility. It would be a wonderful life.

"No," I answered.

My family had a lot to absorb and there was stunned silence for a long time until mom looked up at me. "Why not, Luna? This is your inheritance."

"I don't want it," I answered.

"You need to think about this more, Luna," Chad replied. "I don't think you fully understand what this could mean for you. You own a freaking winery in Italy!"

"I don't want it!" I yelled and ran upstairs.

I was laying face down on my bed and crying when Chad walked in. I knew I was being childish. He sat down next to me and touched my shoulder. I slowly turned and sat up.

"I'm so sorry," Chad said. "I shouldn't have said that."

I grabbed a tissue and wiped my eyes. "It's okay. I've just been thinking about all of this non-stop for days and I really just want it to all go away. I want to go back to normal."

"But that's the thing, it will never be normal again," Chad replied. "Whether you go there or not, you are still the heir to a fortune. A fortune so vast that none of us in this house, this town or this state could ever comprehend."

"I know. That's what makes me sad, too."

"There must be a way to compromise," Chad said calmly. "It can't be all or nothing."

I took Chad's hand. He was so calm and reasonable in a crisis. I knew including him would help bring a new perspective to my drama.

"Plus, you're rich!" Chad smiled. "You know, my car's been acting up..."

I punched his shoulder and he stood up. We both laughed and he looked at my unopened luggage still on the floor. A neon sign that I still hadn't dealt with anything from Italy.

"So, you and Antonio are serious?"

"I don't know," I answered honestly. "We want to be, but I really don't see it happening."

"Well, I'm here if you need me," Chad said, "for anything."

I knew that. I have known that fact for as long as I have been alive. I remembered all of the times he had ever helped me. When I was learning to ride a bike, tie a shoe or whistle, it was always with Chad. My big brother next door was always there when I needed him.

Chad gave me a hug and then looked into my eyes. Even though we had been in each other's lives for so long, I would never take this man for granted. He was too important to me.

LATER THAT DAY WAS Jenny's housewarming party. I was looking forward to it and was glad that I hadn't missed it. I showed up at her door with wine, a Christmas cactus plant and my laptop. I planned to give the same presentation.

First we got a tour of the house. Jenny had lovely furnishings and it was in a great neighborhood. There was a fire in the fireplace, a decorated tree in the front window and she had made a delicious lunch. I just couldn't relax.

I smiled and laughed but the whole time I was anxious about how they would react to my news. Unlike with Chad and my parents, I hadn't mentioned anything about what was in the will. This would be their first time hearing any of it.

When they asked me questions about my trip I simply told them I would fill them all in later. Well, after lunch and some drinks, it was later. I went to get my laptop.

They knew about my trip in August, since they helped me with the bogus email. I would start today's presentation from five days ago. Their expressions were the usual shock and then smiles. Then I showed them the pictures.

"Oh Luna, when you live in Italy, I will come to visit every month!" Jenny said.

"I can move with you and be your personal secretary," Trish added.

Nancy looked at me. "What are you planning to do?" She asked.

"I'm not going."

There was a brief moment of confused expressions before they all started talking at once. They thought I was crazy, wrong and in denial. I probably was a little of each, but I still didn't want to go.

It wasn't until after everyone calmed down that we had a real discussion. I was open to hear what they thought, in fact, I welcomed it. These were women who had nothing to gain or lose from my decision. They were just looking out for me.

"Don't you see how much good you could do with your new position?" Nancy asked. "You could take care of your family, they wouldn't have to work. You sister could go to college anywhere in the world. You could even live part time in Italy and have houses anywhere else you wanted."

"It's not about the money," I replied. "I didn't ask for this."

My friends were trying to explain to me that this didn't have to ruin my life, it could make things better for everyone. I never started this journey wanting any of this, all I wanted was answers, not a piece of the fortune.

"But I could still do that and stay here at home. I could have a normal life in Erie and forget any of this ever happened," I said. "I can let Marco buy me out and never look back."

"Then what?" Trish asked. "Be just another rich person in the world? You would have no position or power, just money. You have to really think what would make you happy?"

That really was the number one question, wasn't it? What would make me the happiest? I was happy in Italy, but I'm happy in Erie, too. Would my rejection of Vernetti Vineyards also be a rejection of Cosimo?

I was so happy when he acknowledge me as his daughter, why was I afraid to step into that role? I was scared, but this was also a gift from my father. He didn't have to include me in the will at all, but he did. I was a Vernetti.

I tried to enjoy the rest of the evening with my friends, but I could tell they acted differently around me. I kept insisting I was the same person.

"But you're really not," Jenny said. "You might trick yourself into thinking that, but you aren't."

"We still love you, though," said Nancy.

They all came over to give me a group hug. They said that nothing would tear apart our friendship, not even a hot Italian man. It was nice to hear, even if we knew things were changing. I just hoped it wasn't irreversible.

We tried talking about other people and topics, but the conversation always came back to Italy. I suppose it always would. I promised I would take everything they said into consideration, but we all knew it was ultimately my decision.

When I got home that night, my head was spinning, literally. Between the wine and the conversation, I just wanted some peace and quiet. I took Bear for a walk before turning in for the night. It had stopped snowing and had turned into a nice evening.

Chad came out when he saw me walk by his house. He asked if I wanted company. I would never refuse him. Personally, I think he was the one who wanted company. The quiet house still bothered him.

"Hey, did you ever ask out that new teller? What was her name, Doreen?" I asked.

"I did, but she already has a boyfriend," he replied.

I felt bad for him. Chad had always been unlucky in love. I knew there had to be someone out there for him, but maybe she wasn't in Erie. I suggested he try online dating and he laughed.

"No, thank you." He said.

I laughed, too. It was worth a shot. We walked a couple of times around the block before returning to our homes. I waved goodnight and went inside. Dad was watching football and I joined him.

"Who's winning?" I asked.

Dad just smiled. "Does it matter? You don't even know who's playing," he answered.

It was true. I tried to understand the game once or twice, but to no avail. It was just one more thing that showed our differences. When I remained quiet, he turned to me.

"How are you doing, my little moon?" He asked.

"I'm okay," I replied. "How are you handling all of this?"

"Oh, it doesn't matter to me one way or the other," Dad insisted. "I just want you to be happy. If that includes running a winery in Italy, then great. If not, then that's great, too."

I put my head on his shoulder. I could always count on my father to make things seem simple. I liked that he didn't try to push or persuade me. He wanted me to make the right decision for me. He was just being a dad and making sure his little girl was happy, just like Cosimo was.

Chapter 27

Christmas morning was a welcomed distraction. I could get caught up in the magic of today and not have to be reminded of Italy at all. We went to Mass and then came home to open presents. It was nice to just be a happy little family, again.

Mom got dad an iPad, it was something he had been hinting about for months. Dad got mom gold earrings and she put them on. Alice opened her gift of designer boots and she loved them. Mom handed me my gift next.

I opened the box to find a new leather purse. It was red with two shoulder straps. I loved it. When I set it on the floor, she told me to look inside. There was a small package tied with a faded blue ribbon.

When I untied the ribbon, I saw that they were letters addressed to Shirley Grant, mom's maiden name. Mom came to sit beside me and whispered, "These are from Cosimo." I touched each one delicately, as if they would disappear in an instant.

"They are yours now." Mom added.

Mom had given me all the correspondence that she had from Cosimo. Finally, a missing piece to my puzzle. These letters, in his own words, could provide some of the answers he couldn't when he was alive.

I put them back in the purse, I would read them later. Now was not the time. Today was supposed to be no reminders of Italy. It took all of my will power to push them to the side.

We had invited Chad over because we didn't want him sitting at his house alone during Christmas. He never grew up with the same reverence for the holiday as I did, so we liked to include him when we could.

We spent the rest of the morning preparing for our Christmas meal. The house smelled amazing, the ham was almost done. The dining room table was set for five and the side dishes were already in place.

Christmas music was playing, the tree was lit and the gifts were opened. It was turning out to be a nice, relaxing Christmas. There was a knock on the door and dad let Chad in. We all started to bring more food to the table dad was carving the ham, we were ready.

Another knock on the door made us all stop what we were doing. Chad was closest to the door, so he opened it. The man outside seemed confused.

"I'm sorry," the man said, "is this Luna Delaney's residence?"

Chad stepped outside to prevent him from coming any closer. "Who's asking?" Chad raised himself to his full six foot frame, but I called to Chad to let the man enter. Even though he was a bit unrecognizable with a winter hat and scarf on, I knew that voice.

"Antonio!" I yelled. "What are you doing here?"

Everyone looked at the man who was now standing in our kitchen. He was slowly peeling off his many layers of outerwear and was soon recognizable as the man in my pictures. This was Tony.

Chad, still unsure of Tony's intentions, tried to stand between him and my family.

"It's okay, Chad," I said. "Tony, come in. We were just about to sit down and eat."

Mom hurried herself to find another chair and readjusted the place settings. Tony sat next to me and opposite Chad and Alice. Mom and Dad were at the heads of the table. It was quiet and awkward.

Dad was the first one to break the silence. "What brings you here, Tony?"

"This," Tony replied. He held up my journal in his hand. I had completely forgotten about it.

"But I asked you to mail it back," I said, surprised.

"I was going to. But when I was filling out the envelope I realized I missed you too much and decided to deliver it in person," Tony answered. "I'm sorry, I wanted it to be a surprise."

It was. My family slowly warmed up to Tony, except for Chad. I would often catch him staring across the table at him. I gave him a kick under the table and he stopped.

Tony said this was his first real American meal. He had traveled to New York City once before, but they always ate in restaurants. He gave his complements to the cooks and seemed to be right at home. I took his hand and smiled at him.

I could see that it would be impossible now to have a day without thinking of Italy, not with Tony here. He said he could stay a week and we insisted he stay here.

Actually, Chad had offered him a bedroom at his house, but I thought that might not be the best idea right now. The couch pulled out to a bed, that would be fine for now.

After dinner, I offered Tony a choice of pumpkin or apple pie. He wanted to try both. I still couldn't believe Tony was sitting next to me, but I was actually starting to feel happy that he was here.

After dinner, I could tell Chad was eager to go back to his house but I stopped him before he left. "Wait," I said. "I haven't given you your Christmas present, yet."

He tried to protest, saying he didn't expect anything but I gave him the present anyway. I watched Chad unwrap the journal. He stared at it and thumbed through the pages. "Thank you," he said.

"I've realized how helpful they are when you have no one else to tell your secrets and feelings to. I wanted you to have that outlet, too." I replied. "At least for the times I'm not here."

Chad smiled and gave me a firm hug. I understood what it meant to him. He kissed my forehead before releasing me and going back home.

Later, when Tony and I were alone in the dining room, he asked me how everyone took the news. I said they thought I was crazy that I didn't want to go.

"What? You don't want to go?" Tony asked. His expression was one of confusion. "You will turn your back on Italy and the Vernetti's?"

I looked into his eyes. I knew he also wanted to ask if I was turning my back on him, too. "I just don't know," I answered.

He dropped the subject but I could tell he didn't want to. He still had so many questions and wanted to persuade me to go back. I certainly knew he would use the next week to try.

"Oh, I almost forgot!" Tony said. He pulled a small velvet bag out of his pants pocket and put it into my hand.

Inside was a beautiful gold bracelet inset with small diamonds all the way around. It was the most beautiful thing I had ever seen. He took the bracelet from my hand and secured it to my wrist.

"Merry Christmas," Tony said.

"Thank you," I replied as he kissed me.

"I just wanted you to remember me," he said.

How could I ever forget Tony? He was constantly in my thoughts. Now he was even an important part of my decision making. I was determined to not let Tony influence my ultimate decision, though. I had to do what was best for me.

We enjoyed the rest of Christmas Day. After all the gifts were finally opened, we relaxed with drinks around the television and watched Christmas movies. This was not something Tony had ever done, so it was important for me that he felt included.

Mom had mulled wine, dad had a beer and the rest of us had rum in our egg nog. When the news came on later, I nearly spilled my drink when I saw the local reporter talking about an accident on Upper Peach Street.

"Jenny!" I yelled.

Everyone turned their heads to see Jenny, bundled up and holding a microphone explaining that Peach Street was closed around the mall due to a five car pileup with injuries. She looked great, a natural. Jenny had made it on the news!

I explained to Tony that she was one of my best friends. Friends that he would be meeting soon. I had already texted them all and we were meeting up in a couple of days. I was anxious, he was excited.

I tried to relax, but I was still finding it incredibly difficult to believe that Tony was sitting in my living room. Five weeks ago I was sitting in his and then meeting his family, now it was reversed. I could no longer ignore Italy.

AS SOON AS TONY AND I walked into the restaurant, my friends smiled. They had never seen me with a serious boyfriend, especially one that flew across the Atlantic Ocean to see me. Tony hugged them all and then sat down next to me.

I had to admit that Tony looked amazing. His hair was a bit longer that it had been in November. The dark curls were starting to cover his ears. He had some facial hair, but he kept it cut close so it was little more than stubble on his lip and jaw.

I realized I had missed him very much. The time I had spent with Tony in Italy were some of my happiest moments. He showed me that he could be a compassionate listener and a faithful friend through all of my drama while I was in Italy.

Watching my friends interact with Tony was interesting. He laughed at their jokes and really engaged with them. My friends seemed to be behaving until Tony asked a question that I knew I would not like to hear the answers to...

"What was Luna like growing up?" He asked.

Trish, Nancy and Jenny all looked at each other and smiled. I, however, was afraid of the childhood stories they were about to bring up. I was right.

First, Jenny told Tony about the time I got a bead stuck up my nose. She also was happy to share the time someone pulled the fire alarm at school and she told everyone it was me. I was in trouble for a week after that.

Nancy told Tony the story about how I lost my car keys in the sand at the beach. We spent three hours looking for them until I finally found them. It had started raining, so the three hour search was all during a downpour. Tony laughed a lot at that story.

Trish surprised me. Her story wasn't one of embarrassment, hers was about the hours we spent on the phone when her mom was sick and she just needed someone to talk to. Or the times when she wanted me to come over to help when her dad was still at work. We would turn the music up to dance and make her mom laugh.

I looked at Trish and squeezed her hand. Tony was beginning to see the bond we really had. There were fun, stupid and silly stories, but the ones that made us friends all of these years were the times that we were there for each other, that's what really mattered.

We were all silent for a minute until Jenny called the waiter over and ordered shots to toast Tony. We all took the small glasses and toasted, "To Tony!"

The conversation was easy and light after that. No more deep and burning questions about who I was, but they were all still curious about one thing.

"So, Luna, are you going back to Italy with Tony?" Nancy asked.

They all looked at me, including Tony. I really hadn't considered it. I knew Marco was still waiting for an answer and he wouldn't wait forever. I had just never thought about when I would go back, if I went back at all.

"I don't know," I replied. "We haven't discussed it." It was the truth, we hadn't discussed anything about our future. I knew what he wanted but I didn't know what I wanted, yet.

After dinner, we said our goodbyes to my friends. Tony said he like all of my friends and I knew they liked him. The numerous texts I received from all of them afterwards proved it.

I drove Tony down to the dock. We parked and watched the lights move on the water from the car. We did have things to discuss and now was a good time for it.

"Luna, I love you," Tony said.

"I love you, too."

"Then why are you hesitating about starting a life in Italy?" He asked.

I had to admit, my reasons were slipping away, fast. It was much easier to deny wanting to go back when Italy was thousands of miles away. Now Italy was sitting right beside me.

I looked down at my hand in his. "I don't know anymore," I replied.

With his other hand, he raised my chin so we were looking into each other's eyes. He kissed me. It was quick and gentle as we sat in the front seat of my car. Too cold to go outside and sit, we stayed in the car and kissed again.

This time his kiss was asking, no, begging me to come back to Italy with him. I could envision it when I let myself. We could get a house in Rome or build a house out near his grandparents. There was also that house in Frascati that was mine.

Chapter 28

Life was full of choices. We can choose to be safe and walk the paved pathway. There was a peacefulness in knowing that our footsteps were secure and that we would arrive at our expected destination. The easy route of least resistance could be a great life for some people.

It's like when some people go to the same destination for their vacation year after year. It's pleasant and predictable. There was nothing wrong with choosing to stay on one path your whole life. But there was so much more out there in the world.

Another choice involves risk. We could turn towards the overgrown path, but that needed courage and patience. We could put our safety, or peace of mind and even our heart at risk just for the possibility of a better life. We could go somewhere that we have never been before. That was risk. Risk challenges us to try new things and go new places.

Each footstep, in either direction, was a statement about ourselves and who we wanted to be. I could stay in Erie, find a wonderful job and have a safe life with my friends and family. I could see it and believe it. That life was right in front of me, until Tony came here.

The life that I saw now was one of risk and following the overgrown path. I may stumble and fall multiple times but I knew I would have someone next to me the entire way. Tony loved me and I loved him. It could be worth the risk of the unknown.

I had called my friends and explained my decision. They all claimed to have already figured it out even before I did. It had only taken them minutes after seeing Tony and I together for them to guess I would be moving to Italy. No matter how much I protested and claimed indecision, they knew.

Chad was harder to convince that I was doing the right thing. He was less trusting of people, that was understandable. He had been let down by everyone, except me. Even though I felt like I was abandoning him, he would not stand in my way to give it a try.

Chad liked the safety of the paved walkway with the signs pointing him which way to turn. He wanted life to be predictable because he had grown up with so much instability. For Chad, having security in life wasn't a choice, it was his lifejacket.

IT WAS NEW YEAR'S DAY when we boarded our flight to Rome. I had packed the things I thought I would want right now and left the rest. My heart pounded as the plane backed away from the gate. Tony squeezed my hand and it helped.

I had decided to go for it. I had to give it a try. Cosimo had given me this gift, this opportunity to be a part of the Vernetti family and I needed to honor that. I was literally flying into the vast unknown territory of wealth and expectations, but I would not be doing it alone.

I took a deep breath, closed my eyes and prayed. I didn't expect it to be easy, but I had started this journey looking for answers and now that I had them, I felt stronger. Maybe it was a false assumption to think I could just walk in and handle all of this, but I did.

Fear would probably always be inside of me to some degree. I just wasn't going to let it stop me from walking down the path that I had chosen. I would no longer allow myself to be told which path to take, this was me taking my life back.

The flight seemed extra short, even though I knew that wasn't possible. I was eager to see where this new path would lead, but it would be baby steps at first. Fear was telling me that I could always turn around and go home. But as I looked at Tony sitting beside me, love was telling me to stay.

AT TONY'S APARTMENT, we settled in as best we could. It was soon clear that this place would not be big enough for both of us long term. It was fine when I was staying with only a small suitcase for a week, but this was different. This stay could be indefinite.

"We will make it work," Tony said. "Until we find another solution. I can move my things into my father's place to give you more room."

I insisted he didn't need to do that, but he did anyway. It would only be a minor inconvenience, he said. I let him do what he needed to do. I didn't mind, as long as we were together.

I let Marco know that I was in Italy and to say he was pleased to hear it would be an understatement. He wanted to know exactly when I would arrive in Frascati so he could be ready. I hesitated. I wanted to enjoy a few days in Rome before I put myself in Marco's hands.

"No problem," Marco insisted. "Come on Monday. It will all be arranged."

I spent the weekend driving around Rome on the back of Tony's scooter. It was easy to forget why I was really there. We picnicked with bread, cheese and wine in the countryside, we toured ruins and we went to numerous museums.

Tony showed me a side of Rome that most tourists don't see. He took me to see his friend who played guitar in a small band. They were playing at some little restaurant on the outskirts of the city. It was fun to see this side of Rome, this side of Tony.

He made me believe I could really be happy here. There was still one thing I needed to do and that was to go shopping for a new outfit or two. Tony as happy to take me to the best stores. I had never bought designer clothes before, unless they were thrift store finds.

I was meeting Marco and the family soon so I needed to look the part. It took browsing in several different store before I finally put together several outfits, shoes and accessories. It was still cold, so I also needed a warm coat to complete the ensemble. I had never spent that much at one time ever in my life before.

Tony approved of all my purchases while I had mild heart attacks at each price tag. Marco had wired money to my back account, I had just never used any of it until now. I didn't know how I would ever get used to buying whatever I wanted. Tony just laughed.

Throughout the weekend we visited many places. We ate in nice restaurants and also from street vendors. We had sandwiches from walk up windows and pastries from glorious bakeries. It was hard to pick my favorite food so I tried them all.

My favorite place, though, was eating in his restaurant while sitting with Tony and his father. It was during one of those evenings when his father talked about his wife. After thirty years of marriage, she passed away a couple of years ago. It was a heart attack that took her quickly.

The two men, still feeling the loss, became quiet. His father said he could still feel her presence, that was why he enjoyed spending all of his time in the restaurant.

"She is here," his father said.

Tony touched his father's shoulder and nodded his head. The pizza arrived and the food helped lighten the mood. It was crispy and delicious. The Vernetti wine was also wonderful. These two men had been through a lot and made it to the other side.

The restaurant was a success and they lived right next door. Their lives have revolved around this tight community. I still wasn't sure if Tony and I would be living in the same place in Italy. My responsibilities would be in Frascati and his were in Rome, an hour away.

I didn't want to dwell on all of the obstacles we would be facing, there would be too many to even list. There would even be obstacles we haven't even considered yet that would stand in our way. It would be up to us to figure a way through them.

I knew we could do it. I had to trust that this was going to be worth it for all of us. I felt calmer. I was giving myself permission to enjoy the moment and not worry about the struggles we would face in the future.

Marco sent me another message informing me that the press were invited on Monday. I was glad for the warning. This was a big day for Vernetti Vineyards. Speculation had spread throughout the country as to who would be stepping into Cosimo's footsteps.

Some assumed it would be solely Marco, other's doubted that the empire would rest on a teenager's shoulders when there were other, more capable, family members. Cosimo, with no siblings, had uncles and extended family. What they didn't know was the existence of me.

The estate kept all details related to the will private. No news had escaped of a daughter who had inherited half of everything. This would be a shock to the country and the tabloids would have fun with this news.

My hands started feeling sweaty as I held my phone. I put it upside down on the table and took a deep breath. Tony asked if there was bad news.

"Not exactly," I replied and told him Marco's news.

Tony and his father just advised me to stay strong and smile. They would try to delve into my past and dig up dirt, but there were no skeletons buried there. I sent a quick text to all of my friends and family back home. All I could do was warn everyone that we were entering the public eye.

I had no frame of reference for this sort of thing. Tony thought it would blow over just as fast as it came in. I wasn't so sure. There was scandal in an American inheriting the winery, a beloved Italian icon. This was sure to be a hurricane rather than a gentle breeze.

Back at Tony's place, I tried to remain calm. I packed my bag with a few days worth of outfits, just as Marco suggested. It was all of my new designer clothes along with some of my more casual favorites. I didn't want to completely lose my identity.

Tony packed a bag, too. He was always nicely dressed, even though it was mostly black, gray and white clothing in his wardrobe. I had tried to get him to purchase more colorful items during our shopping trip, but he refused.

I showered, changed and laid down in bed. I felt calm, there was no need to worry about something I had no control over. I pulled out my journal, the one that Tony personally flew over to deliver, and wrote down what happened today.

It was hard to believe the stories this journal housed. What started as a quick visit to tie up loose ends has developed into a life changing adventure, one that was by no means finished. In fact, one could say it was only the beginning.

The wooden box from Cosimo was still sitting in Tony's dining room. I had brought the letters that mom gave me and I sat in bed to read them. I never really had a chance since Christmas because Tony had come and manipulated all of my time.

Now I had a quiet moment to devote to the letters that my biological father had written to my mother, presumably about me. Tony walked in to see me crying in the middle of a sea of paper. I wished my mother would have explained all of this to me sooner.

The letters talked about his wanting all of us to be together, but couldn't. He wanted to be involved in his daughter's life but his family would never allow it. He told my mother that the day I was born was one of the happiest in his life. He would spend his life making it up to her and to me.

This was when he changed the way the company was run, no more dark dealings in shady offices. Vernetti Vineyards would be a name that people looked up to, not feared. Even the label on the bottles reflected the new look with a new moon. An act of defiance to his family was a proclamation to the world. A secret hidden in plain sight, Luna was on the label and in his heart.

Chapter 29

Marco had arranged for a driver to pick us up at nine in the morning. The drive was pleasant but inside I had knots in my stomach. The fear of the unknown was encroaching on my calm. I tried to focus on Tony sitting next to me and it helped, a little.

When the driver stopped the car in the circle gravel driveway in front of the residence, I took a deep breath. I stepped out of the car and into the flash bulbs of dozens of cameras that were aimed at me. There were men in black uniforms that were keeping them at bay. I adjusted my coat and walked up the stairs where Marco was greeting us.

Tony joined me at the top of the stairs and we all turned to the cameras. I waved and smiled even though I was a nervous wreck inside. Men in uniforms were unloading our bags and taking them around the side of the building.

Marco and I posed together and then we all turned to enter the residence. I was thankful for the quiet once the large front wooden doors closed but soon realized that there was also press inside the building.

"These are our own photographers," Marco explained. "We don't allow the public inside, so we choose what we want them to see."

The photographer took a few candid photos of me and Marco together and then some more of me alone. We had a meeting to get to, so I would come back later to finish taking more pictures. Right now we had more important things to do.

Marco led the way into the large meeting room, again. This was the same room the will was read in. I was hoping the room might have a different atmosphere, but there were even more people sitting around this table today. Marco explained that they were all staff.

In fact, I learned today that I had my very own assistant. His name was David and he was Cosimo's assistant until he passed away. David was a middle aged man and had been with Cosimo for twenty years. He loved the family and was extremely loyal.

"We couldn't just let David go," Marco explained. "So we asked him to wait to see if you would be joining us. We are very thrilled that you are, so is David."

David stood up to introduce himself to me then gestured for me to take the empty seat between him and Marco. I did. The ladies and gentlemen around the table were very welcoming, as any group of twenty strangers could be. They also stared at me as if betting on how long I would stick around.

I could guess that the odds weren't good, but I was going to prove them wrong. I could be as loyal and trustworthy as any of them. I stared right back. I tried to read what everyone's body language was saying about them. They looked as if they were ready for a battle.

The group discussed old business and tried to fill me in on where certain plans stood and the progress of each item. I took notes, as did David. When they got to the new business, I quickly learned that I was the focus of everyone's attention.

They were going to run a new wine label. The first major change since Cosimo took over and added the full moon to the label twenty-three years ago. The mystery of that change was only now coming to light, but the new change would be adding Luna's name to the new blend.

They were already toying with the idea of a new blend, but now it was in full production and it was to be called, 'Luna'. It would still have the moon on the label, but now it had a name. I was shocked and honored when this news was met with murmured approvals around the room.

It was clear that everyone in this room had loved Cosimo and they were willing to transfer some of that love to me. The rest I had to earn. There were prototypes and samples offered around the room. The new blend was like nothing I had ever tasted from Vernetti Vineyards before.

I loved it. At least they weren't proposing to put my face on the label! I could handle my name being on billions of bottles. It was still surreal to be holding a wine that was named after me. There were just some things I would never get used to.

The next order of new business was the construction of something Vernetti Vineyards had never considered, until now. Marco explained that public interest was growing after Cosimo's death. The public wanted to know what would happen with the company.

Vernetti Vineyards had been open to the public, to a degree. They offered wine tours, tastings and even hosted special events such as weddings and parties. They were now moving forward with a restaurant.

This was new territory for the winery. They all agreed that this was a cautious first step to a possible hotel in the future. The restaurant would offer a top notch menu, delicious desserts and, of course, a full Vernetti Vineyards wine list.

Marco turned to me after the restaurant presentation, "And we want you to oversee the building and operation of the restaurant, Luna."

I instantly felt the blood drain from my face. I knew nothing about the building or operation of anything, let alone a multi-million dollar project. I had a marketing degree, not anything that would help me with this project.

When I didn't answer right away, Marco added, "Don't worry, we have a team of professionals lined up to do the work, you will be the liaison for the company at future meetings for updates. David will help you with anything you need."

I still wasn't convinced that I was the right person for the job, but I nodded my head and they moved on. I was no longer the topic of their next item of business which was good because I felt faint. Luckily David was still taking notes, I would ask him for the highlights later.

We took a break for lunch and I was eager to see Tony. He had spent the afternoon reading in the library, again. He wasn't invited to the meeting, but he was okay with that. I, however, would have loved for him to be sitting next to me.

As we were escorted into the dining room for a buffet lunch, I filled Tony in on the new projects. Tony was impressed with the idea of a restaurant here on the property. He thought it would bring in a lot of people.

I had been given a lot to absorb today. During lunch, I tried to enjoy the food and the surroundings, but my mind kept going back to what was expected of me. It was clear that, for now, I was expected to stay in Frascati. Tony would have to go back to his life soon, too.

After lunch, Tony was invited to enjoy the game room, piano room or even the kitchen if he liked. I was to go back into the meeting with Marco. He was apologetic and said that meetings don't usually run so long, there was just so much to discuss with my being here.

The meeting concluded with a few more details discussed and approved. David said he would be in his office if I needed anything. I nodded, not even knowing where that was. The whole day had come and gone in a blur.

We found Tony in the piano room and Marco asked us both to sit down. He had one more item to discuss with both of us. Marco went on to explain that the restaurant should be completed very soon.

"How soon?" I asked.

"In a couple of months," Marco replied.

I looked at Tony, impressed. I had never known construction jobs to be completed so fast, but then I never knew one that was backed by so much capital.

"My question to you, Antonio, is," Marco began. "Would you like to be head chef?"

Now Tony looked like he had seen a ghost. Up until now, I had been the only one dealing with surprises being thrown at me left and right, now Tony had a life changing offer. I took his hand as if trying to bring him back to the present.

"That's a very generous offer, Marco. I feel like I need to think on it for a bit," Tony replied.

"Of course, there is still time to make a decision," Marco answered, but we all understood he had a limited window. If he accepted the position, he would have a home here in the residence.

Now Tony had the blank stare of uncertainty. This was a big decision, indeed. His restaurant was in Rome. Would he give it up to move here? What about his father? Would Tony give it all up for me or not?

He had spent months telling me to come to Italy for him. Now I was asking him to make a similar move and sacrifice for me. Could he do it?

Marco said that our bags were delivered upstairs and perhaps we wanted time to be alone. I nodded and he led the way up the grand entryway staircase. We went up one more flight of stairs and then down a long hallway.

"The family's rooms are down this wing. Guests are on the opposite wing," Marco explained.

I had no idea how many rooms there were in this house, but I was sure we could accommodate a small army if we had to. Marco led me to one door and Tony to another door and returned back down the hall.

I turned to Tony and giggled, this was unreal. We each entered our respective rooms. Mine had a large bed with a deep green comforter. The curtains were in the same matching green material. I went to the windows and saw that they faced out to the vineyard. From this vantage point I felt like I could even see Sicily.

I ran my hand along the ornate desk, chairs and dressing table. I couldn't believe that this would be my room. There was an adjoining room that I noticed had bookshelves, a tv and a writing desk. My private quarters were grander then I could ever imagine.

There was a knock on my door. I opened it and let Tony in. He said his was just as grand, but no adjoining room. His had a dark blue comforter and curtains. I saw that he still had a troubled look and I went to hug him.

"Listen, I understand if you don't want to move here," I said. "It was a big decision for me and it's just as big of a decision for you."

"Trust me, I want to," Tony said. "I just need to find a way to explain it to my father. We've never been apart."

I completely understood. It was just the two of them now. Even if Tony sold the restaurant and his father stayed there, he might get lonely. Bringing him here, where he didn't know anyone would also be lonely.

"But you really want to come here and be the chef?" I asked.

Tony kissed me. "Yes, I want to be on this journey through life with you."

We made love under my green comforter that night. Tony never stayed in his room and I secretly think Marco suspected this because Tony's luggage was left right next to mine at my door. Marco was just being a gentleman by offering Tony his own room.

I liked Marco. He was well mannered but also a nice guy. He was also my brother, my only family in Italy. It's not that I ever forgot it, since we looked so much alike, I just liked reminding myself that I had a brother in Italy.

Chapter 30

The first night in my new home was amazing. With Tony by my side, I felt like I could do anything, even build a restaurant. At least now, I wasn't the only one with my head spinning. When I caught Tony in moments of deep thought, I would put my hand on his shoulder.

It was a comfort to know that we were there for each other. I opened the curtains and took it all in. I couldn't believe the twists and turns my life had taken to bring me to this place in time. Sometimes I felt like I needed to pinch myself. So far, the risk was worth it.

Marco said we were free to explore for the day. We were to meet up for dinner at seven tonight. We had access to the vineyard, winery and the golf cart vehicle. It was too much land to explore in one day so we spent most of our time in the winery.

We watched how it was made and bottled, even helped out along the assembly line. The cellars fascinated me the most. Barrel after barrel of wine just resting until the right time. I had a lot to learn but I was willing to start now.

We took a couple bottles back to the house with us. There was a lunch set up in the dining room and we sat down at the long table, just the two of us. We felt like little kids left alone for the day whose parents wouldn't be home for hours.

After lunch we walked from room to room, discovering areas we still hadn't seen yet. I ran into David and asked him to show me his office. He led me down the wing that was directly under our bedrooms. He showed me his office first, then mine.

Mine was twice the size of David's and although it had its own entrance, it was also connected to David's by a single door. I sat down at what would eventually be my desk and looked around my office.

It was grand, or course, but empty. It was a blank slate waiting for me to put my personal touch on it. I would start by having mom send over some of my things from home. Thinking of home made me a bit sad, I would not be returning there anytime soon.

That feeling of being overwhelmed started creeping in, again. Just as Tony was getting over his feelings, mine were starting to come back. I didn't know any other way of getting past them then to just keep pushing through them.

I tried focusing on my immediate needs. I needed to find out exactly what I'd be doing, where Tony would be living and when I could get started. I wasn't afraid of the work, I was just concerned that I would be a disappointment.

Tony, on the other hand, was delighted to get started. The idea of creating a restaurant from the ground up with a professional staff, state of the art equipment and at Vernetti Vineyards was not difficult to agree to. He was downright giddy with excitement.

Tony and I dressed for dinner and went down to the dining room. It was just us three, presumably the staff ate elsewhere. Marco asked how our day was and we said we had a wonderful time exploring the grounds and winery.

He was pleased that we found everything satisfactory. Tony and I laughed, it was breathtaking. We thanked him for his hospitality.

"Luna, I want you to know that you are welcome to move in permanently anytime that is convenient for you," Marco said. "This is your home now. I will be staying at my father's house on the other side of the vineyard."

Luna remembered that house well. The one she visited when she first came, where Cosimo died. It was also the house where she cried on the steps along with her mother twenty-three years earlier.

"Thank you, Marco." I replied.

"You are welcome to stay as well, Antonio," Marco said. "There are other quarters for staff who wish to live on the property, but it is up to the owner."

Marco gestured at me. I was the owner of this palace. I smiled at Tony and confirmed he would be living here with me. Marco smiled and nodded. We could move in immediately.

The meal was wonderful and it was followed by dessert. I put my fork down and looked at Marco.

"You know, your father didn't really want me in his life. He had turned his back on my mother when she told him she was pregnant with me. His uncles threatened her and tried to pay her off but she wouldn't take the money. Plus, he was married." I said.

I wasn't really sure why I said it. I wasn't trying to shock Marco or change his opinion of his family. I guess I just didn't want any secrets. If there was anything to be dug up by reporters, it could be this. Marco simply looked at me and leaned back in his chair.

"My father knew his family was doing bad things on the side. His father and grandfather used the winery as a way of covering up their darker businesses. My father wanted to change all of it. He cleaned it up so that the family name could be respected, again. No more mafia connections, my father wouldn't allow it," Marco said.

"I'm sorry about what happened back then with your mother. Especially since he and my mother divorced only a few years after I was born. Perhaps his only love was your mother," Marco continued.

"By then, my mother had already met Ron," I said. "I think she was trying to put Italy behind her. There are moments I feel like I'm betraying her, by being so willing to come back and be Cosimo's daughter."

"No, it is not betrayal. It is righting a wrong that was done to her. I think by putting the moon on the bottle was a sign to the world that you were his. He was just waiting for the moment that you would see it," Marco replied.

I did see it, one ping only.

"I wished I had met you sooner," I said.

"Me, too," Marco replied. "It would have been nice to have a sister around."

Talking about family made me miss mine. Marco was all alone and so was I. I was starting to feel closer to Marco and I think Tony was warming up to him, too.

We walked to the library after dinner where there was a fire in the fireplace. I could picture myself curled up here on the sofa in my robe and slippers with one of the thousands of books from the shelves.

Tony and I sat in silence for a moment, staring at the fire. It was our first night here as residents of the house, no longer invited guests. Marco, who had stayed here in case we needed anything, would return to his own house tonight.

I called my parents to fill them in on what had been happening the last few days. Every detail sounded strange in my mouth as I told them everything. I asked for a few items to be sent and that it would be awhile before I came back to visit.

I had also asked Marco to wire money to my parents for me. Until I found a financial person to handle my accounts, I relied on Marco. I asked dad to go to the bank tomorrow and check their account. I wanted them to finally be comfortable in their newly retired life.

They were silent for a moment until the realization of what I had just told them sank in. They didn't need to work anymore. I think Cosimo would be happy with the fact that the woman he once loved was finally getting some recognition.

I told mom that I had finally read her letters. I understood things so much more now that I had both sides of the story. I missed Bear and hoped to get back soon once the restaurant was up and running. Maybe things could settle down a bit after that.

Next, I texted Chad. 'Are you up?'

'How's it going?' He asked.

'I feel like a princess in her castle,' I replied.

'Good,' Chad said.

I gave him a brief recap of the last several days. I said how Tony would be the new chef at the restaurant I was building. It still sounded so foreign to say it out loud. I asked how things were going at home.

'Okay,' Chad replied. 'Mom has to move out. Her sister doesn't want her there anymore. I'm not prepared for her to move back in with me. I don't think I could handle that anymore.'

I understood why that would be too traumatic for him. The years of childhood mental abuse he suffered, not to mention physical abuse would be impossible for him to willingly allow into his life again. My heart ached for him. I prayed for Chad each night, full moon or not.

Tony and I continued to sit in silence, both lost in our own thoughts. I grabbed a Jane Austen book from the shelf and curled up against Tony's shoulder. I knew he was still considering how to tell his father that he was moving to Frascati. I just hoped he would be able to do it.

Eventually we made our way upstairs to my room. We were both tired after a long day wandering the grounds. I knew he had to go back home soon to have a talk with his father. It was weighing on him and he wouldn't be able to relax until he had the hard conversation.

"I'm going to head home tomorrow," Tony said.

"I know," I replied. "I pray that everything works out fine. Then, come back to me." Those were the words he had said to me when I went home. Now I was saying them right back.

Tony kissed me. "I will," he promised.

These were the words I wanted to hear and I hoped he was sincere. There were expectations on him now and it would be easy for anyone to get cold feet. He could go home and decide to stay there and continue with the safe road, just as I did at first. I would never blame him or make him feel guilty if he chose that path.

These choices are what define us and show our true character. I had believed that the safe and easy life was what I truly wanted but Tony showed me there was another way. It may be filled with risk, but anything worth trying had some risk involved. I probably would have never come back to Italy if Tony hadn't taken the risk and flew to Erie.

I would have to trust that the choices Tony would make would involve me. I know now how he felt when I left Italy and wanted to stay home. Now I was letting him go home to make up his own mind where his future would truly be.

I wanted a future with Tony, even if that meant a life of risk. I just needed to find out if that was what he wanted, too. I slept uneasy that night. There weren't any dreams of a girl in a blue dress.

This time she was in outer space looking down at the earth and moon who were drifting apart from each other. There was no more gravity holding them together. The moon was spiraling farther and farther away until there was a faint whisper.

The girl was surrounded by noise and had to really strain her ears to hear it. Then she heard the words clearly, the whisper was saying, 'Come back to me'. The girl looked and looked for who was whispering those words until she realized it was her.

Chapter 31

Antonio returned home to Rome. He had a lot to think about and discuss with his father. There were the easy solutions such as selling the restaurant and renting out his apartment full time, but he had his father to consider.

I knew Antonio's father would not move out of his home, even for a more comfortable life in Frascati. To him, life wasn't meant to be comfortable. Life was meant to be felt, whether it was pain or joy.

I felt comfort and joy at the vineyard. I wasn't sure that I would, which is probably why I resisted for so long. How could I want to live in a house that represented so much pain for my mother? But I did, I felt a real connection here.

It was difficult to describe and I don't know that I could properly articulate it to someone else how I felt a history here, even with never stepping foot in this house before August. It was like I had been here all along. Maybe I have, maybe my father kept my spirit alive here for me.

I didn't know how long Tony was going to be gone. My own acceptance and eventual return took months. I would let him take all the time he needed to make his decisions and arrangements. Taking a new path in life, even at twenty-nine, would be a test of anyone's spirit.

I couldn't just sit around and wait, though. According to Marco, we had work to do. I spent days out at the construction site talking to the people in charge of the project. Things were moving fast and it looked fantastic.

There was plenty of outdoor space with seating during the spring and summer months along with ample indoor seating to practically accommodate the whole town. There was also a venue in the upper levels for catered events and entertainment.

They could host small classical or headliner concerts, they could host community events and so much more, the possibilities were endless. The rooftop bar would probably be my favorite space of all. Guests could literally spend a whole day here if they included a tour of the vineyard and winery in their day.

When Marco had mentioned future expansion that included a hotel, I was sure this would be a destination, not just a day trip for Italians. I was excited for what the future held for Vernetti Vineyards and I was proud to be a part of it.

I met with David every morning. It was clear that he had been doing this his whole life and it was easy to stay on task with him around. I had a tendency to give in to the chaos when I started feeling stressed and David's calm demeanor would keep me on task.

Things didn't always run smoothly, though. I was trying to make do with my own laptop and notebook, but it was becoming increasingly difficult to manage the massive amounts of emails and paperwork.

Marco was always reminding me that I did have a business account, a budget as well as a personal account that I had access to. He advised me to get some proper office equipment so that I wouldn't fall behind. He was telling me nicely to get my act together.

Up until now I had been calling on Marco and his financial advisor in order to keep track of all the accounts. Marco said that I had access to any personnel I required to make life easier for me. I considered the options Marco presented and was still unsure how to proceed.

I was sure that everyone Marco provided was wholly capable, reliable and trustworthy. I wanted someone who could not only oversee my income, expenses and accounting, but could potentially aid Tony with his. There was really only one name that came to mind.

'Are you up?' I texted.

'How are you doing?' Chad asked.

'Things are going really well,' I replied. 'How are you, though, did your mother come back?'

Chad went on to explain that his mother did return even after repeated attempts to get her to stay in Pittsburgh. She showed up with her bags and guilted him into letting her stay. He was miserable with her home. He never did have a close relationship with his parents, now it was tested to its limits.

'Chad, I need you here,' I texted. I went on to explain that I needed someone I could trust. He would have a comfortable place to stay, a job and a pretty sweet working environment. 'Plus, I'm here.'

Chad laughed but then stopped. 'You're serious?' He asked.

'Yes, this is not a joke,' I replied. There was silence while I waited for a text back. There wasn't any. 'Think about it. I'm offering you a new life, if you want it.'

I put my phone down and pictured Chad staring at his phone. This was a big decision for him, I understood that. Life was a series of choices, there was never just one big one. Letting his mother move back in was a choice. I was simply giving him another option.

I knew it was a long shot. Chad never once in his life mentioned wanting to leave Erie, in fact he said he didn't want to many times. That was when he only pictured the safely paved trail that he followed in life. He had walked right past the overgrown path that I had taken. Now it was visible to him, too.

I really had no idea which way Chad would be leaning, would he want to get away or stay home and keep moving forward. I could only hope for one but expect the other. I went to bed feeling a little unsteady. The two guys that I cared most about in this world were both making the toughest decision of their life right now. I was afraid they would not take the risk.

All I could do was wait. That was the hardest part, knowing there was nothing I could do to help either one with this decision. It had to be theirs and theirs alone. If they were going to come here to live and work, they had to decide for themselves.

AFTER A COUPLE OF WEEKS, it was Tony who replied first. He said plans were in place to sell the restaurant to his cousin. This was the best possible outcome because his cousin had secretly wanted it and never said anything. When he let his family know that it may be for sale, his cousin jumped at the chance.

Tony's father wouldn't have to move and could still visit the restaurant anytime he wanted. He didn't want to give up his apartment, though. He would rent it out full time and suggested that my own family and friends could use it when they came to Rome.

I was so happy for him. I could hear relief in his voice when he called. He wanted to come to work for Vernetti Vineyards, but I also knew he wouldn't abandon his father or see his restaurant fail. This was fantastic news and also a wonderful compromise.

The staff got Tony's room ready for him to move into. He would be given a room similar to mine that had an adjoining work space. He would be arriving in a few days and I couldn't be happier. Things were finally falling into place.

I couldn't wait for him to get here. I kept myself busy with the restaurant, but now that the building was finished, it now needed to be furnished. Tony would be hands on when it came to completing the kitchen and the dining rooms.

The day Tony finally arrived I ran down the hallway to meet him. I jumped into his arms and kissed him right there in front of the staff that were carrying his belongings to his room.

"I've missed you," I said.

"I've missed you more," Tony replied.

Tony would have an office downstairs like I did but his would be near the back of the house with easier access to the restaurant. He wanted immediate updates about everything related to the building. David and I were happy to oblige.

Tony was in his element and his enthusiasm was contagious. His eyes lit up when talking about stoves, ovens and warmers. He made sure there was plenty of cold storage, freezer space and storage rooms. Some days I wouldn't see him until dinner time.

Marco was impressed with the progress of the restaurant and thought we could announce the grand opening in March, which was next month. I was a mixture of anticipation and anxiety when the opening day was looming so closely overhead.

Tony was in charge of hiring the staff, creating menus and making sure things ran smoothly. He hoped to have enough trusted managers in place that his plate could become a little lighter once the restaurant opened.

There were taste tests to be performed, seating arrangements to be made and decor to approve. I liked walking through the main dining rooms to picture what it would be like to be enjoying a meal here. The floor to ceiling windows took advantage of the view out onto the vineyard.

The restaurant was charming, elegant and peaceful. Tony had done a wonderful job, as I knew he would. He caught me watching him one day and he smiled.

"You look happy," I said.

"I am happy," Tony replied. "Thank you for this."

"You did this," I answered, gesturing with my arms. "I only gave you the choice."

It was true, I simply offered him to walk this journey with me and see where it would lead. The path was still a bit overgrown, but we were foraging a trail. I could never have guessed that a random booking of an apartment six months ago would lead to having the man of my dreams right here by my side.

I was going over the numbers for the new 'Luna' wine. We would be launching it the same time as the restaurant opening. Marco had already envisioned the new wine before I came on board, so I just had to help it across the finish line. The 'Luna' blend would be the first new wine that Vernetti Vineyards would have produced in more than a decade.

The wine had already been leaked to the press to draw a buzz along with the grand opening of the restaurant that would be called 'Cosimo'. It was fitting that the one thing that had brought us all together would be named for the person responsible.

Marco said he had a surprise for me at the grand opening. He wouldn't give me any hints, just that he was sure I would love it. I asked a dozen questions about what it was but Marco just smiled. Despite persistent pleas, he would not say anything more about it.

Fine, I would wait. It seemed like I was getting better at waiting for things to happen. I had called my parents and gave them the usual update about what was happening around here. I asked them to come, but dad wasn't feeling well and it would have to wait. They were sorry but promised to come as soon as they could.

Even with all the excitement of the new wine and the grand opening, I would miss having my family here to celebrate with me. It was during milestones like this that they would normally make sure they were by my side. There would be other occasions, I was sure, but I still felt the emptiness.

The text I received next would change all of that.

'Are you up?' Chad texted.

'Hey, how are you doing?' I asked.

'Same, mom is here now,' he said. 'It's not working out.'

I knew that wasn't good. I wished there was something I could do or say to help him, but there wasn't much from so far away. All I could do was listen and try to cheer him up.

'I really wish you would consider my offer,' I said. 'I know it's frightening to take such a big leap of faith, but I did it and I don't regret it. Is there anything I can say to help you make this decision?'

Chad hesitated. 'No, because I'll be there in two days'.

Chapter 32

When Chad arrived at the house, it felt like the most natural thing. It was as if he was always meant to be here with me. Marco had sent a driver for him and his room was ready. His eyes were large and observant as we showed him around the palace.

"I'm going to need a map to find my way around," Chad joked.

"That's what your phone's navigation is for," I replied. We laughed and hugged. My earth had arrived.

Chad had meetings with the financial team to go over the books. He felt right at home talking numbers and making budgets. I still couldn't believe he was here but I was thankful to have him on our team.

We were able to sit together in the library one evening when Tony was still at the restaurant applying finishing touches. Chad was still in awe of his surroundings but put his arm around me.

"I'm so proud of you, my little moonbeam," he said.

"Thank you," I replied.

"I mean it. You took a chance and you made it work. Not many people would do that," Chad said.

"Maybe not, but I know two guys who did just that," I replied.

Chad nodded. He and Tony followed me down the overgrown path and it was worth it. Chad had chosen to lift himself out of the pit he was in. There really was no other way for him to go, he had needed a hand.

We sat watching the fire in the fireplace. Just being together was enough. We weren't the kind of friends who needed to fill the silence.

I was glad his days of sleeping on my fuzzy rug were finally over. Now his life could begin.

It was the day before the grand opening of the Cosimo Restaurant and Marco requested us all to come to the entry way of the residence. It was a welcoming space that had a large round table in the middle of the room with fresh flowers daily. The room also opened up to a double staircase that led to the second floor.

There were paintings, portraits and tapestries that adorned the walls of the massive room. It was the kind of entry way where you didn't know what to look at first. Your eyes were trying to take it all in at once and you just couldn't.

Marco stood next to a large easel covered in a cloth. There was a large assembly of people I recognized only from meetings and passing in the hallway. They all stared at the white cloth with anticipation. I assumed it had something to do with the opening tomorrow.

I was wrong. When Marco lifted the cloth with as much fanfare as a magician showing his greatest feat, I was stunned. Marco revealed a large portrait of me.

"I couldn't wait to show you all, especially Luna," Marco said. He explained that this was painted by our portrait artist who had done many of the ones we saw in the hall. The artist had used one of the photographs from the day I arrive in January. The photographer, Gia, was also there to admire the portrait.

There were murmurs around the room about how beautiful and life-like it looked. It was a beautiful painting, even though I was embarrassed by the subject matter. Gia came over to shake hands and said that I was very photogenic. I smiled and introduced her to Tony and Chad.

Chad couldn't take his eyes off of Gia. I smiled thinking that he had just found another reason to stay. We all went up to get a closer look at the painting. It was stunning how it looked so real. Tony kissed me and said that it was gorgeous, just like me. I rolled my eyes.

Marco said that because it was to be hung later today, Gia was there to take pictures to send to the press. Gia took photos of me with the painting, then added Marco. Later she asked Tony to be included and even Chad. It seemed that he had caught her eye, too.

Tonight, everyone ate in the restaurant. It would be a dry run to see how things went before the public was invited tomorrow. It was the first time I had seen it in a couple of weeks and it was breathtaking.

A man was playing the grand piano in the corner, the lights were on low because candles were lit at every table. The smells were amazing coming from the kitchen. We sat at a table next to the window. Marco, Tony, Gia, Chad and I enjoyed the 'Luna' wine and proposed a toast.

"To Cosimo," I said to which they all repeated.

"To Luna," Marco said and they all repeated.

It was a long day. I let myself enjoy the moment of great wine, delicious food and wonderful friends around the table. I squeezed Tony's hand and touched Chad's arm. I couldn't be happier. It was clear, however, that Chad was more distracted by Gia.

The only thing missing was my family. They assured me that they would come soon. They were working on last minute paperwork, plus, Alice didn't have a passport. I knew it took time to get everything ready, I just missed them all.

THIS WAS THE DAY THEY had all worked so hard towards, the grand opening of the Cosimo Restaurant and the official rolling out of the new 'Luna' wine. It felt like I had just given birth to twins. Both were a lot of work but each was very rewarding.

With the restaurant not opening until eleven o'clock, I spend a quiet morning with Tony at breakfast. Tony opted to wear a crisp, white chef's coat and uniform today. I pulled out one of my designer outfits for the occasion. There would be press here, so I needed to look very professional.

There would also be lots of people curious to see and examine the new addition to Vernetti Vineyards, both me and the restaurant. This would be everyone's first chance to meet me in person. I noticed in this morning's papers we were front page news.

Chad had come down to join us. I passed him the newspaper when he sat down with his food. He smiled and nodded.

"You are very photogenic," Chad said.

"That sounds just like something Gia said," I teased.

"Oh really?" He answered and winked at me as he ate.

I sat back in my chair and reminded myself how lucky I was. I looked at these two guys at the table and I felt instantly calmer. I felt like I could tackle anything with them by my side. I may just need all the support I could get to get through today.

As I walked out into the main entry way, I paused to look up at the portrait of me that was hung yesterday. It looked like it has been hanging there for years, like it belonged there. I smiled and we all went outside to the restaurant.

The parking lot was full and there were already people lined up. We had started taking reservations a month ago and it booked up quickly. Tony was eager to open the doors.

The rush of people entering the restaurant were orderly but constant. Tables were filling up and it was getting busy. It was wonderful to watch. Tony took a page from his father's book that said to always leave a table available for family. This table was in the corner by a window.

Marco made the rounds and welcomed everyone who came. Everyone knew Marco but it was me they were curious about. I followed Marco and then he let me go off on my own. I was learning Italian, but I was not at all fluent.

All they really wanted was to shake my hand and take a picture with me. I could handle that. After a couple of hours mingling with everyone, I went into the kitchen to check on Tony. He was completely hands-on and calling out orders. He was sweating, busy and happy.

It was obvious how much he loved cooking. The food looked and smelled delicious. He looked up and saw me watching from the doorway. He smiled and waved and I did the same. I didn't want to disturb him, so I went up to the rooftop deck.

This was where people who didn't have a reservation came just to see the restaurant. Guests were still welcome to order a drink or appetizers and walk around the deck. There was seating, but with a 360 degree view, who could sit in one spot?

The weather was cool and cloudy but there wasn't any chance of rain. That was good for March in Italy. This was a great way for people to get a feel for the place and then make their reservations for the spring, summer and fall.

I was being recognized everywhere I went. I couldn't even count how many pictures were taken of me, but it had to be in the hundreds. I didn't mind, this was worth it. I went back downstairs to look for Chad.

I walked back through the restaurant and out onto the outdoor patio. There were a few people here, but I didn't see Chad. It wasn't until I turned the corner to go up the back stairs that I saw him with Gia. They were standing by a tree and talking.

I was about to turn and go back inside when I saw him lean down to kiss her. I smiled and left them alone. Today was a big day for all of us. I quickly went back inside to join Marco.

It was only noon but it felt like midnight. I made my escape back into the house and went to my room. After kicking off my heels, I curled up on my couch and opened my book. I didn't realize I had dozed off until there was a knock on my door.

It was Tony. The lunch service was winding down and would be transitioning to dinner soon, so he wanted to check up on me.

"I should be checking in on you," I said. "You looked busy but very happy."

"I am," he replied and sat down next to me. "I realized when I looked up and saw that you had left the kitchen that my life would be so empty without you. When you walked into my life six months ago you altered it forever."

I sat up and hugged him. We were both getting emotional because I felt the same way. Our lives collided and that's how we want them to stay. I am incomplete without him.

"I love you," I said.

Tony didn't reply right away, he just looked at me and smiled. When he went down on one knee my hands went to my mouth. I didn't know what to say.

"Luna, I love you more than anything in this world. Will you make me the happiest man alive and marry me?" Tony asked. He pulled out a small velvet box from his pocket and opened it. Inside was a sparkling diamond ring that he took out and held in front of me.

"YES!" I yelled. "I would love to marry you!"

Tony sat beside me, again, and placed the ring on my left hand. The image blurred as my eyes filled with tears. We hugged and kissed and then I looked at the ring, again. I never expected this to happen, not now. I knew I wanted a life with Tony, but I didn't know if he was ready.

"When do you have to get back to the kitchen?" I asked.

"I don't," Tony replied and we stayed in the rest of the afternoon.

Chapter 33

News of our engagement spread fast. My picture was already a daily occurrence in the newspapers and magazines, now it was even more so. People loved the idea of my marrying Tony, especially Marco, who already considered him part of the family.

Chad had warmed up to Tony, too. They actually spent time together on their days off going to play tennis or golf. Sometimes we all took trips into Rome or to the ocean. We took Gia, too, of course since she and Chad had started dating.

We all tried to maintain a healthy balance of work and relaxation. Tony trusted his managers and chefs to run the restaurant so that he could play tour guide with us. We explored parts of Italy even Tony and Gia had never been to.

"Where should we get married?" Tony asked.

"I don't know," I replied. "Where is the most beautiful place?"

"You need to get married at Vernetti Vineyards," Chad said, matter-of-factly. "How could you consider anywhere else?"

I had thought about it, but I wasn't sure it felt right. Tony was from Rome, I assumed he would want to have the wedding there.

"Why not Rome?" I asked.

"Frascati is our home now," Tony replied.

It was not something we had to decide now, we could wait a little longer. My family was coming over in April and I was very excited to see them. It seemed like a lifetime ago that I left home on New Year's Day with Tony. There was so much to show them.

Even Alice was coming. I wasn't sure if she would, but mom confirmed that her passport came and they had bought her a ticket. It would be nice to see her and get her opinion on this place. I knew that she would fall in love with Italy.

We were all learning more about Gia. She was from Rome, as well, and from a large family. She had been a photographer for Vernetti Vineyards for four years and they have been very good to her. She did other photography jobs on the side, but she didn't need to, Gia was busy enough with the winery.

Gia had mentioned wanting to visit America, then looked at Chad and suggesting meeting his family. Chad simply shook his head and said that there were better things to see than home. I knew Chad never wanted to visit his home again.

I was sure that Gia would never meet Chad parents, they were no longer a part of his life. He was embracing his new life in Frascati and enjoying the freedom of having a real relationship. Gia could show him places he had only dreamed about. That made me happy.

We drove back to the vineyard and Gia went home. Tony went to check on the restaurant and Chad went to his room. I walked into the library and called my friends. I hadn't had a chance to tell them about my engagement, so I was eager to give them a call.

We did a group video chat and they were so excited for me. They wanted to come and visit but would settle for a wedding invitation. I didn't know when it would be, yet, but I would let them know soon.

They filled me in on some of the local news from home. Trish had met someone and Nancy and Jenny approved of him, so that was good. I was so happy that things we going well with everyone and couldn't wait to see them.

I saw Marco walking down the hallway and he stopped when he saw me in the library.

"I've been looking for you," Marco said. "Congratulations! I haven't been able to say that to you in person, yet."

"Thank you," I replied.

"Have you decided when you will have the wedding?" Marco asked.

"I haven't even decided where," I answered.

"Here, of course!" Marco said sternly. To him, there was no question it would be at the vineyard.

I tried to protest, but he insisted that it be held here. In fact, August would be the perfect time, but that was up to me.

"August? Do you really think that's enough time?" I asked.

"Sure, all you need is to make a list of people, find a dress and the rest is simple. We have weddings here all the time!" Marco said.

August would be rather perfect. It would be exactly one year since I met Tony. What better way of celebrating our love then getting married a year later? I told Marco I would discuss it with Tony and let him know.

"Great!" Marco said.

I could tell that having the wedding here made Marco happy. He was probably thinking about Cosimo and how he would have loved being a part of it. I was pretty sure Tony would agree to having the wedding here, especially after our conversation earlier.

I smiled when I thought about all of my family and friends here and how it would look all decorated for a wedding. I didn't want to wait, August would be perfect.

I did discuss it with Tony later that night and he was completely onboard for an August wedding at Vernetti Vineyards. I asked him to provide a list of guests when he had the time. He seemed so busy lately.

Tony enjoyed helping out in the restaurant. He would cook the fish or chop onions, it didn't matter. He loved the atmosphere and getting his hands dirty. He didn't have to put in so many hours each day, but he enjoyed it.

"I will work on it tomorrow," Tony said.

"I will get mine ready, too," I replied.

"Are you ready to be Luna Gabriella Rossi?" He asked.

"Yes."

THE ANTICIPATION OF my family arriving today had made it very difficult to eat or sleep the last couple of days. I had considered going with our driver to the airport to meet them, but there was so much to get ready here so I stayed. I would have a grand welcome for them.

I had double and triple checked their rooms so that they would have everything they needed. They would be staying in the family wing of the house. I wasn't really sure what they all thought about staying here, but I was glad they agreed.

I knew it would be hardest for mom to drive onto the property. She wasn't allowed inside Cosimo's house the first time she was here. Dad knew the whole story now and he wasn't as hard on the family. If they hadn't said no, he would never have met my mom.

Alice was the most neutral. Technically none of these people were her family except those flying with her today, and me, her half-sister. Alice would be making up her own mind about whether she would accept them or not.

I had tours and trips planned for their visit. I made sure that Tony and even Chad were able to come on some of them with us. Chad was also eager to see my family, it was a piece of home that he actually missed.

But it was Marco who wanted to make a good impression the most. He understood how difficult his family had made my mother's life when she needed help the most and wanted to make up for it personally. I insisted that a nearly twenty year old did not have to accept the guilt of an entire family. Marco just simply smiled.

I saw that Marco had put champagne in my parent's room along with chocolates, fruit and drinks. They were even bringing Bear. I would never admit out loud that it was Bear I was most excited to see, but I had bowls of food and water all over the house.

Tony came downstairs to check on me. I tried to eat breakfast but I only had coffee. He, on the other hand, was hungry and ate beside me.

"How are you doing?" Tony asked.

"I just can't believe they are actually coming here today," I replied.

"I'm so happy for you," he said.

He gave me a hug and I checked the time. They should be arriving any minute. I wanted everyone to be at the front entrance waiting as they pulled up. Tony finished breakfast and walked with me down the hall. Chad was already there.

Marco came to let us know that his driver informed him they are approaching the driveway. Just as we stepped outside on this warm and sunny April day, the car pulled up into the circular driveway.

My eyes were filling with tears in anticipation of hugging my mom. She was the first to get out of the car and come to me followed by my dad and Alice. They all hugged and shook hands with Tony, Chad and Marco.

Mom was crying. "Oh, Luna," she started.

"What is it?" I asked.

"Bear," Mom said and continued crying.

"Where is Bear, mom?"

"He didn't make it," Dad answered for her. "He passed away last week."

Mom came to hug me again and explained that they had all the vet paperwork ready for Bear to travel, but as the weeks went on, he go so much weaker. I knew he was old, but I wanted to see him one last time. He could have lived out his last days in luxury.

Chad was wiping a tear away, too. He had grown up with Bear as well. It was the worst news for me to hear, after expecting to see my dog jump out of the car. I hated that this was how we would start our reunion, but Bear was more than a pet, he was my best friend.

I tried my best to focus on the fact that my family was standing in front of me. I couldn't believe that Bear wasn't with them. The staff took their bags to their rooms so that we could take them on a tour. We started with the house, since we had breakfast waiting for them.

The first thing they noticed was my portrait in the entry way, even Alice was impressed. Mom hugged me and kept looking at everything from floor to ceiling. She had never been in the main house. Dad just nodded and kept following Tony and Chad to the dining room.

They said they weren't very hungry but it gave us a chance to sit and catch up a little. They were enjoying their early retirement and were taking the time to take road trips and do some remodeling to the house they had been putting off.

It made me happy that I could help ease their burden a bit. Dad said he even bought a boat and enjoyed fishing on the lake most mornings. I could picture him out there no matter the weather. Maybe now he could actually catch something.

Alice was on spring break but the school year was almost over. I told her she should come and spend the summer with me. Her face lit up when she accepted my offer.

"I would love the help in the restaurant," Tony said.

"I could use your help going over the ad campaigns for the summer season," I added.

Alice couldn't contain her excitement. It was important to me that she felt included in this side of my family. This was a side she had no idea about, the same as me and I didn't want her to feel like I was choosing one over the other.

It was while I was showing my family to their rooms that I spent a few minutes alone with Alice. She was rightfully impressed by the ornate decorations of her room and the entire house.

"It really is like a castle," Alice said.

"Maybe more like a palace," I replied. We both laughed but the opulence couldn't be denied.

"Are you happy here?" She asked.

"Yes, I have Tony and now Chad to keep me company," I replied.

"And Marco," Alice added. "He's cute."

"Ew, no!" I responded. "He's my brother and your my sister. Stop!"

Alice just laughed. "Okay, I'm sure there are plenty of other cute Italian boys around here."

I rolled my eyes. I would have my hands full with her if she came back for the summer, I could already tell. I gave her a big hug and kiss on the top of her head. I loved Alice and wanted her to feel welcome. We were all family now.

Chapter 34

It was fun for me to show my family all that Vernetti Vineyards had to offer. I took them on a tour of the vineyard and the winery. Dad was not a big wine drinker, but we all sampled the new 'Luna' blend and they loved it. Even Alice had a taste.

Tony wanted them to have dinner at the Cosimo Restaurant, so the family table was set for us. He brought dish after dish to our table. Everything we ate was amazing and there was no way to choose a favorite.

After dinner, we went up to the rooftop and had our dessert. It was the perfect place to see the sunset over the vineyard. I could tell mom and dad were starting to relax and really enjoy themselves. Alice kept looking at all the cute Italian boys.

I had made arrangements for Tony and Chad to come with us to Rome for a few days at the end of their trip. I didn't want them to come all the way to Italy and not see more than Frascati.

Tony was the best tour guide and was happy to oblige. We took them to all of the tourist sights and they were impressed everywhere we went. Besides, they were seeing Rome for the first time and there were certain places you just couldn't miss.

We took our time driving and walking from one place to another. We would see the colosseum in the morning and then have a long lunch at a lovely outdoor cafe and people watch. I wanted them to not just see Rome, but to experience it. Do as the Romans do, wasn't that the old saying?

Our days were filled with afternoon breaks and late dinners. We took them to Tony's old restaurant and met his father and cousin, who now ran it. We all sat together and had tuna pizza. I loved seeing our fathers interact and play charades since they didn't speak the other one's language. It didn't matter.

We had spent a day shopping, too. A trip to Italy wouldn't be complete without shopping. They didn't want designer clothes, but a new purse or shoes wouldn't hurt. Dad followed Tony's advice and bought a new leather jacket.

We took lots of photos on the Spanish Steps and at Trevi Fountain. We all threw coins in so that we could have good fortune and return to Rome someday. Alice wanted gelato, so we all made our selections and sat outside the Pantheon.

Mom especially loved Vatican City. We didn't have time to tour the Vatican Museum, that would be for next time. Instead, we walked inside St. Peter's Basilica. It was nice, after a busy few days, to just kneel down and have a quiet moment. I could sit here for hours but we had more places to go.

I hoped that my whole family would come for the summer and stay as long as they wanted. I loved having them here with me and watching them embrace my fiancé and my new life was priceless. I was sad they had to go home tomorrow.

We spent out last night at Tony's old restaurant. We had drinks and dessert and it was clear that no one wanted to leave. Mom was already tearing up at the thought of going home. I insisted that they were welcome to come anytime and stay as long as they wanted.

Tony offered his old apartment if they'd rather stay in Rome. They thanked us both for the generous hospitality but it was me who was thanking them for coming. Mom had waited until now to present me with a gift she had brought.

"I had been putting off giving you this, but I can't wait any longer," Mom said.

She handed me a little blue velvet jewelry bag and I emptied the contents in my hand. It was a silver necklace with a pendant. At first I thought it was something she bought here in one of the shops, but no, this was different.

As I took a closer look at the pendant, I noticed it was in the shape of a paw print with some kind of stone set in the middle.

"It contains some of Bear's ashes," Mom said.

I was so emotional as I looked from the necklace and then to my mother. I had never seen anything like this before and I was struck by how thoughtful the necklace was.

"He will always be with you," Mom added.

I gave her a hug and cried. I didn't want them to leave, but I knew they had to. This has been the most perfect week and I wanted them to stay. We made a toast to Bear and then headed back to the hotel. It was late and I knew they had to pack.

I told them I would see them in the morning and gave everyone more hugs. In our room, I just wanted Tony to hold me and tell me everything would be okay. I felt his calm and comfort and was able to have a restful sleep.

The next morning, at the airport, I tried to stay positive. I kept reminding myself that they would be back. They had to come for the wedding in August if not sooner. I could wait four more months. I still cried, though.

I was quiet the whole ride back to the vineyard. I had a wonderful week with my family and couldn't help but replay the weeks' events in my head. I was sure they had a good time, too. Chad was quiet. I didn't know what he was thinking about.

"Are you up?" I asked.

Chad smiled at our familiar phrase. "I'm good," he replied.

"Just making sure," I said.

He put his hand on my shoulder from the back seat to let me know he appreciated me. I don't think either one of us could ever completely comprehend how much we needed each other. We both had gone through a lot and came out the other side relatively unscathed, at least on the outside.

Chad and I were there for each other when the whole world was against us, or so it seemed. All those years of supporting each other bonded us in a way that couldn't be explained. Tony was starting to understand it, but not really. He wasn't threatened by Chad, though, and that's all that mattered.

Going back home also meant getting back to wedding plans. I had hoped we could have squeezed wedding dress shopping into my week with mom, but that would have been too much to ask. Marco had insisted on have a designer brought to the house.

Tony and I had finished our list of guests. Mine had a grand total of thirty, although I was sure only about ten would come. Tony had a larger family, so his had seventy-five names. Marco added another fifty that included family, friends and staff. It was a big event, he kept reminded me.

"Just to be on the safe side, we will round it up to two hundred," Marco said at dinner.

"Round up?" I asked. "Usually at weddings we round down."

Marco laughed. "I can assure you more people will try to come to this one."

I wasn't sure what kind of ominous statement he was trying to make. I was sure my friends would come with a guest and my family. I had asked Chad if there was anyone he wanted me to bring over for the occasion and he simply said, 'no'.

I asked my friends to come a week early so that we could hang out before the wedding. I wasn't sure what plans we had after the wedding, since Tony said the honeymoon location was a surprise. I wanted as much time with my friends as possible.

Alice came as soon as school let out for the summer. She wanted to help and was given tasks at the restaurant. She was still too young to be at the winery, but she loved playing hostess, waitress and prep cook in the kitchen.

Alice would go where ever she was needed. For her, this wasn't just a summer vacation, it was an internship that she hoped would turn into a full time position. She didn't want to go back. This statement made me nervous because I knew that wasn't part of the deal.

She was to come here for the summer and then go back to finish high school. It was her senior year. She offered to transfer or do homeschooling. She begged to stay. I said I would think about it but it was my parent's final decision.

It was still a few weeks before the wedding when Tony came into my room. I had taken the afternoon off and was listening to music. With the wedding plans, work at the winery and now Marco saying that we would be moving forward with plans for the hotel, I needed some alone time.

Tony hesitated at the door, which I thought was strange. He wasn't working today and had on shorts and a polo shirt. He opened the door a crack and spoke to someone else in the hallway. Curious, I narrowed my eyes and gave him my compete attention.

"I brought you a helper," Tony started. "She insisted she would help with wedding plans and I think she will also make you smile and relax."

I could tell Tony was amused by this vague description of who ever, or what ever, was behind that door. I, however, was getting more anxious.

"What is it?" I asked.

Just then, Tony opened the door completely and out from a box that Chad had been holding in the hallway came this tiny brown puppy. The puppy ran to me but stopped to sniff everything along the way. I bent down to scoop up the little bundle of fur.

I held up the puppy to look into her little face. It was a Bolognese puppy that needed a name. I let her lick my face and then turned to face Tony.

"Thank you," I said.

"It was Chad's idea," Tony said. "He knew how much you loved your dog. I just knew where to go to get one."

I walked over to Chad and Tony and gave them each a hug. The puppy sniffed and licked them, too.

"What will you name her?" Tony asked.

"What's the Italian word for a bear?"

"Orso," Tony replied.

"Then her name is Orso," I answered.

It was wonderful having a dog around again. I took Orso for walks around the vineyard and even over to the restaurant. Everyone wanted to take Orso out, even Chad. I could hear him talking to the little puppy and wondered what deep, dark secrets they shared.

Orso was pampered by the staff, it was clear that they hadn't had a dog inside the residence before. As Orso grew, so did the affection around the vineyard for her. Alice even took her out when she had errands to run around the property. I hadn't realized how hard Bear's death was on Alice until I considered that Bear had been in her life since she was six.

My parents were planning to come two weeks before the wedding so they could help me get ready. I didn't tell them that I didn't need any help. I did want them to feel included so I would give them tasks to make them feel useful.

I was feeling very emotional knowing that everyone I loved and cared about would be there to watch me get married to Antonio Rossi. It was more than I could ever hope for. I could never have dreamed that my life would turn out like this a year ago.

A year ago I had discovered my mother's secret that she had hidden from me for twenty-two years. That was when I saw C.D.V.

on a small dot in Italy on my computer screen. How my life had changed by taking that chance!

My father stopped at the front and kissed me then gave my hand to Tony. I walked up to Tony and stood facing him. I knew that I would never have to face anything alone every again. I stared into his eyes and it felt like we were alone, even though two hundred people were watching us.

Tony was the wild card in this whole scenario. It was by chance I met him and rented his apartment. He took the chance and offered to show me around Rome. We each took a risk that day and we were glad we did. I never knew how it would change my life.

Some may say it was already written in the stars, I have to say it was probably in the moon. The ceremony went by in a blur. I know we spoke to each other and exchanged rings. I wiped a tear from his eye and he smiled.

Nothing mattered before this moment, the only thing that mattered was our future. This was it, the moment was here. I felt Tony put his hands on my cheeks and the minister say the magic words, "You may now kiss the bride."

Chapter 35

My parents were the first to arrive a couple of weeks before the wedding. I put them in the same room they had last time. Alice was there to give them hugs and tell them all about her summer. She didn't tell them about her plan to stay, that would come later.

I was able to enjoy the time with my parents without the need to show them around. They knew were everything was and just wanted to relax. Orso was there to greet them, too. Mom insisted on being helpful while dad wanted to see the winery, again.

I let mom go over the flower arrangements with me. I had to confirm with the florist all of the bouquets and centerpieces as well as smaller items on the list. Mom was thrilled to be a part of the planning, however small. She didn't have a big wedding when she married Ron, so this was exciting.

The entire estate would be closed to the public on August 22nd for the wedding. No one would be coming to the restaurant or the winery on that day unless they were invited. Gia was the resident photographer and would handle all of the picture taking that day.

I showed my parents the pictures Gia took for our engagement photo shoot. They had turned out so beautifully. Gia captured the fading light at sunset as we walked along the grape vines. It was such a magical setting and I had felt like a real princess that day.

Marco came over often to make sure I didn't need anything else. My parents liked Marco and he really liked them, too. My mother had tried to sound casual when she asked Marco if his mother would be coming. He simply said, 'no'. He was fully aware that it would be too awkward for both of them to be in the same room.

I took mom to my room to show her my dress. It was custom made by a designer that Marco had brought in. I never imagined anything other than choosing a dress from a bridal store, but Marco insisted that this would be far superior than anything in a store.

It was. When I unzipped the bag that contained the dress, mom gasped. It had lace, beading and satin, everything a wedding dress should have. She would just have to wait to see what it looked like on because I needed a whole team to do that.

Mom teared up when she thought about my walking down the aisle. As I gave my mother a hug, I started crying, too. I was having my dad give me away and Alice would be my maid of honor. How perfect was that!

I had tried to envision my perfect wedding but every time I tried, I knew the reality would be so much better. I couldn't wait to see Tony in his tuxedo with his father as his best man. Chad and Marco would also be standing by his side.

I would have Alice, Trish, Nancy and Jenny. I was extremely lucky to have all of the people I loved with me here. I couldn't wait for them all to arrive so we could start the party.

This was my last night with just my parents and we went out to eat with Tony. Tony knew of a great restaurant that wasn't too far. Their specialty was pasta and seafood. Mom, Alice and I ordered salmon, the men ordered pasta.

It was nice to be sitting around a regular table with my family. I could imagine us back in our dining room at home. It made me a little nostalgic for when life was so much simpler, but also pretty empty.

I could safely say that I felt that my life was full and challenging and that I wouldn't want to change a thing. I wanted that for everyone around the table. Alice finally had the nerve to bring up about her wanting to stay in Italy.

My parents said, 'no', she could come back after graduation if she still wanted to, but she would finish out her senior year. Alice would be returning with them after the wedding, just as planned. I couldn't say I was surprised, nor was Alice. I gave her credit for trying.

I mentioned to her that by then, the hotel should be ready and would need someone with experience to help run it. Alice smiled and nodded her head. I didn't want her to regret not graduating with her friends. I knew how important that could be.

TRISH, NANCY AND JENNY all arrived at the residence and stepped out of the car. I ran down the steps to give them each a hug that quickly turned into a group hug. I was excited to see their dates but was surprised to see that they each had brought their moms.

"Well, when Trish said she was bringing her mom, then our mom's expected to come, too," Nancy said with a laugh.

Each of their mothers stepped out of the car and stared at the house. "It really is a castle," Jenny's mom said.

"No, it's a palace," Trish's mom said.

"It's home," I replied and let them all inside.

They all did the same thing everyone did when they first entered the foyer. Their eyes went immediately to my portrait and then continued looking from floor to ceiling. We walked up the grand double staircase and down the second floor hallway. I gave a brief tour and then led them to their rooms.

My friends would all be staying in the guest wing of the residence. I didn't go down that side very often, so I had to make sure I put them in the right rooms. Trish and her mother entered theirs first. I had champagne and chocolate waiting in all of their rooms.

Across from them were Jenny and her mom. Then, next to Trish was Nancy and her mom's room.

I gave them time to settle in and said that lunch would be ready downstairs whenever they wanted to join us. I would be in the dining room if they needed me. Chad and Tony were already helping themselves.

"I'm sorry, we didn't know how long you would be with your friends," Tony said.

"It's okay, really," I replied. "I told them to come when they were ready."

I was eating with the guys when they all came down to join us. They remembered Tony and were glad to see Chad, again. We all enjoyed a wonderful lunch and my friends went on about how impressed they were with the house.

"Wait until you see the rest of the estate," I said.

They went on about the size, the colors and the decor. I was always amazed how people took it all in the first time they entered this house. I guess I was getting used to it already because I could walk down the hallway full of art and tapestries and not get as distracted by the famous artist's names as before.

Chad and Tony had to get back to work, but I had the rest of the week off to spend with them and my family. I gave my friends the grand tour and then let them relax in the evening at the house. They especially loved the library and couldn't believe it was full of first editions and signed copies.

"So what are the plans for your bachelorette party?" Trish asked.

"Don't worry, it's all planned out," I replied.

My friends and our moms would be joined by Gia at the rooftop bar. Alice wanted to participate, so I reluctantly said okay, I did want her there. I didn't want a wild night out on the town, so I requested cocktails and food and just a lovely evening to watch the sunset. I hired a local band to play and just relax.

Tony, on the other hand, wanted to go out. He took Chad, Marco, my dad, his dad and cousin to a bar in town. He didn't want it to feel like we were spying on each other, so he went away from the vineyard.

They guys had fun drinking at the bar and telling stories about when Tony was younger. My dad and Chad also shared stories of me. I didn't find this out until later, but I didn't mind. I didn't have any secrets left to keep and I wanted it to stay that way.

The two dads tried to communicate. Tony had to translate as best as he could. There was so much my dad wanted to ask Tony and his family, but it would have to wait. Now was a time of celebration. His daughter was getting married.

On the rooftop, we didn't have stories to tell. Instead, the moms were sharing memories of their own weddings. They offered advice and words of wisdom. I absorbed it all. I was so glad that my friends had brought their mothers to my wedding.

Gia had brought her camera and took pictures as the sun set. She took photos of the mothers and daughters and then me with my friends. I didn't need the pictures to remember this night, I would remember it for as long as I lived.

It was a wonderful evening and I was sad to see it end. My mother started yawning and then we all realized how late it was. We rode back to the house and said goodnight to each other.

It still felt surreal that I would be married to Tony tomorrow. Everything was leading up to this moment and I was suddenly very excited for it to happen. Tony would not be coming to my room to sleep tonight. I did want to see him, though.

I heard a noise in the hallway that could only be the guys returning from their own bachelor party. Chad was helping Tony walk down the hall and when they saw me peak out from my door, Tony let go of Chad.

"Hello, darling," Tony said.

"Are you going to be okay tomorrow?" I asked.

"I will," he said.

Chad came over and gave me a hug and a kiss on the cheek. I waved goodnight to him and helped Tony to his room.

Tony wasn't as drunk as I suspected, in fact he seemed almost sober when he sat down on the chair. He looked up at me and said, "I cannot wait until tomorrow!"

I sat next to him. "Neither can I," I replied.

I stayed in Tony's room a while longer. We kissed and professed our love for each other, again. We asked how each other's nights had been and we both said it had been a great night. I reminded him, though, that I wasn't the one who needed help getting back to my room.

He apologized but blamed Chad. I laughed and doubted that Chad was responsible. Orso had come into the room looking for me. I scooped him up and kissed Tony. I would see him tomorrow at the altar.

In my room I had a moment alone to reflect after such a busy and whirlwind couple of weeks. To be honest, it was a whirlwind year. I showered, put on pajamas and climbed into bed. I took one more look at my wedding dress hanging on the door and smiled.

Orso jumped on the bed and curled up next to me. I scratched under his little chin and laid down.

"Yes, Orso," I said. "Let's call it a night."

Chapter 36

Today was the day!

We all went downstairs to breakfast. The ceremony wasn't until noon, so I had plenty of time to eat before I needed to start getting dressed. It would also probably be the only time I would eat, so I relished the food on my plate.

Slowly, everyone made their way to breakfast. My family was there, Tony and his family came into the room. My friends and their mothers looked well rested followed by Chad and Gia. We had invited Gia to stay the night instead of making the drive home and back.

The atmosphere was light and happy as everyone smiled at Tony and me. I couldn't contain my joy, either. I got up to get coffee and offered to bring more to everyone, too. I didn't care who else came to the wedding, as long as everyone in this room made it.

After breakfast, we all went to our rooms to get ready. My mother and sister came to my room to help me with my hair, make up and dress. As the rest of the house got ready, so did I.

The guys were ready first. They walked around checking their ties and hair. The florist was running around the house to pin the flowers on everyone and get the outdoor space ready. There was a team of people setting up chairs and an archway were we would be saying our vows.

The vineyard would be a sea of people when they started arriving shortly. There were people getting the food ready, the place settings and the cake. Someone came in to help with my hair and makeup. I was starting to feel like Cinderella.

My friends would come into my room to give updates about Tony as well as reporting to me how things were going outside. Everyone looked great and Gia was in the center of it all taking photographs.

As the frenzied pace of all the preparations calmed down to a slow trickle, I was able to stand up and enjoy the moment. I didn't get much sleep last night. I was too excited about today.

I took a minute to look at my dress in the mirror. I would never get tired of looking at this beautiful strapless dress with beading on the bodice. There was single strand of diamonds around my waist that transitioned to a satin skirt covered in lace. I had a train but I insisted that it not be longer than a yard.

I twirled in front of the mirror and looked at the back. My mother was now the only one in the room with me. It was nearly time to go downstairs but I wanted this time with just me and her. She had gone through a lot when she found out she was pregnant with me, now she could rest assured that her hard work had paid off.

She helped me put on my veil and I turned back to the mirror. I put some tissues in my pockets and I was ready to go. Mom held open the door and down the staircase we went. My sister was waiting for me at the bottom. Alice looked like a princess.

We were all being led to where we were supposed to be. Mom went to take her seat in the front row. I went outside and found my dad waiting for me to take his arm. It was a warm and sunny day. As we turned the corner to see all of the people, my heart jumped a beat.

There must have been nearly two hundred seated and facing the minister. I saw the procession of Jenny with Tony's cousin, Nancy walked with Marco and Trish walked with Chad. Lastly, it was Alice, my maid of honor walking with Tony's father, his best man.

The music changed and everyone stood up. My father and I stood at the back of the aisle. I could see Tony standing at the front and was watching me.

"Are you ready?" Dad asked.

"I am," I replied.

As we started walking up the aisle, my life was becoming clearer. I wasn't choosing one side of my family over the other, I was sealing them together forever. The Vernetti family, who had once rejected my mother was now welcoming me with open arms. All the sadness and anger from decades ago was now gone.

Each step that brought me closer to Tony made me more sure of every decision that brought me here. I took a chance when I flew to meet Cosimo that day long ago. Just like in the movie, I risked so much to offer one ping to see if he remembered me.

My biological father not only remembered me but build an empire using my name with a wooden box of memories to prove it. Cosimo had given me the life that he wouldn't or couldn't when I was born.

I could see that Tony had tears in his eyes. I didn't, I was walking to him with an open and happy heart. I was choosing to spend the rest of my life with him and I couldn't wait to get to the end of the aisle to join him.

I looked at all of the faces at the front. My best friends were there to support me, no matter what. My little sister, Alice, accepted this new family as her own. Then there was Chad. My earth that kept each of us grounded when it felt like our lives were falling apart. There was no future that didn't include Chad.

Were there tears in Chad's eyes, too? The gravitational pull would always be there, he was truly my best friend. The way he looked at Gia made me smile because that's exactly how I look at Tony.

Chapter 37

We honeymooned in Paris, that was Tony's big surprise. We both had never been. It was a week I would never forget for as long as I lived. We were as busy as we wanted to be, which meant we spent as much time indoors as we did outdoors. Our hotel suite had a view of the Eiffel Tower, which sparkled at night, the perfect backdrop for champagne on our balcony.

I had thought Rome was magical, but Paris could be even more so. We spent an entire day at the Louvre Museum and probably still hadn't seen it all. Tony had arranged a dinner cruise on the Seine and it was like something out of a fairy tale. Being Mrs. Luna Rossi was a dream come true. I never knew a happiness like this!

When we arrived back in Frascati, I knew that I didn't want to live in the palace full time. I discussed it with Tony and we agreed to build a home near his grandparents. I still remembered how idyllic the green grass and pastures were and I wanted that for my kids, not the grandeur of my residence.

I knew Marco had grown up around all of the opulence of the grand and golden homes, but I didn't. I grew up in a three bedroom home with a small front yard and a small backyard. We went to work each day and spent our weekends as a family. We played tag in the front yard.

Tony oversaw the construction of our getaway home and when it was finally completed, we all went out to see it. Our son, Matteo was one year old now and was walking everywhere. I tried to get him to hold my hand, but he would not be told where to go, he was too adventurous for that. I never knew how wonderful it could be to watch your own children grow and explore.

Adventure was in Matteo's genes, as much as Vernetti Vineyards. Matteo Rossi would be next in line to inherit the estate, along with Marco's children. Marco didn't have any children, yet, he wasn't even married. My advice to him was to take his time. He was only twenty-one, he had plenty of time to find the right woman.

Alice did come back after her high school graduation and was working her way up in our new hotel. She broke up with Evan, for her, it was time to move on. The Vernetti Hotel opened on our first anniversary, the following August. It was a huge success and was attracting visitors from all over the world. Alice was in charge of reservations and was a natural.

Frascati was fast becoming a destination and it was exciting to think what could be next. That was when I knew I wanted to put a little more distance between our work life and home life. I loved staying in our residence at the vineyard, but it was even better to get away.

Orso enjoyed playing with the goats and sheep that grazed in the pastures nearby. Matteo loved being spoiled by his great-grandparents with sweets and baked goods. This was the balance that Tony promised when I wasn't sure I could stay in Italy. It felt wonderful to be so relaxed.

Chad proposed to Gia and we were all just waiting for them to set a date. They were so happy and I was happy for them, especially Chad who deserved it the most. He embraced his new life in Italy and was becoming pretty fluent. My earth was finding a new orbit and it felt good. Perhaps Gia was the sun to his earth.

Mom and Dad came to visit often, especially since Matteo was born. I was hoping to have them move permanently over to Italy with Alice and I, but they liked going back to Erie. For them, Erie would always be home. I didn't mind, because it also gave me a chance to come home and see my friends.

For now, things were perfect. I didn't know what the future held for us, but right now I could sit in my back yard that faced rolling green hills and watch my husband and my son catching butterflies with Orso.

It was all thanks to Cosimo who took a chance and gave me a sign on the internet that he was my father. It was that inherited courage that helped me respond. One ping only. I never knew that taking that risk would lead to the life I had now.

Tonight was a full moon and I made a new wish.

My first one had already come true.

Acknowledgements

To my husband, Yoshi, for giving me the time and space to write. To my daughter, Alisa, for reading my first draft and loving it.

To my son, Leo, for his constant encouragement.

To my sister for always being there for me.

To my friends for always being willing to read my first drafts and saying that they were perfect, even when I knew they weren't. Your encouragement has brought me to where I am now.

To Maggie Stiefvater for creating a writing seminar that provided life changing inspiration.

To my parents, who are no longer with us, for their constant love and support.

About the Author

Amy Iketani lives in Stockbridge, Georgia, with her husband and pet cat. Originally from Erie, Pennsylvania, Amy met her husband while working for Club Med and has lived in Florida, Japan and Hawaii. Amy enjoys crocheting, reading, spending time with her two grown children, Alisa and Leo, and traveling with her husband, Yoshi, of thirty two years.

Follow Amy on Instagram @amyiketaniwrites

Don't miss out!

Visit the website below and you can sign up to receive emails whenever Amy Iketani publishes a new book. There's no charge and no obligation.

https://books2read.com/r/B-A-ALFAB-TZHWC

BOOKS 2 READ

Connecting independent readers to independent writers.

Did you love *I Never Knew*? Then you should read *The Last Wish*[1] by Amy Iketani!

[2]

Russell Reed is a widower with a seventeen year old son, Adam. His wife, Lynn, died last summer after a long battle with cancer. The Reed family vacationed at their beach house on Jekyll Island every summer. That is, until last summer, when the emptiness was too much. Now, with Russell struggling at work and Adam barely holding it together, maybe the one thing they have been avoiding is the one place they might start to heal.

Adam sees the girl next door, Mandy, who is now all grown up. She is no longer the little girl with pony tails and braces. Russell must contact the elderly neighbor's daughter, Iris, after she falls. When Iris arrives, she may just be his safe return to love. When Adam finds out

---

1. https://books2read.com/u/3LxeBM

2. https://books2read.com/u/3LxeBM

his father is thinking about selling the beach house, he takes matters into his own hands. Adam's act of defiance turns into a life saving mission of Iris and her mother, Fern. Adam finds his mother's old journal and now believes that the beach house is exactly where they need to be.

The Last Wish is a story of loss and love. Follow Russell and Adam as they maneuver the emotional path of finding a reason for happiness.

Read more at instagram.com/amyiketaniwrites.

Also by Amy Iketani

Coming Home
The Last Wish
I Never Knew

Watch for more at instagram.com/amyiketaniwrites.

About the Author

Amy Iketani lives in Stockbridge, Georgia, with her husband and pet cat. Originally from Erie, Pennsylvania, Amy met her husband while working for Club Med and has lived in Florida, Japan and Hawaii. Amy enjoys crocheting, reading, and spending time with her two grown children, Alisa and Leo, and traveling with her husband, Yoshi, of thirty two years.

Follow Amy on Instagram @amyiketaniwrites

Read more at instagram.com/amyiketaniwrites.

www.ingramcontent.com/pod-product-compliance
Lightning Source LLC
Chambersburg PA
CBHW021151160726
47994CB00001B/148